LITTLE

LITTLE

for careenagers

LOUIS ZUKOFSKY

GROSSMAN PUBLISHERS   NEW YORK   1970

A Note on the Pronunciation of Names

As in Latin: names of two syllables are accented on the first (with a few exceptions, Dríscháy, Uńzúng Phárétte); of more than two syllables, on the penult if that is long (Verchádet, Babállo, Sweetsíder); otherwise on the antepenult (Teárilee, Beármeout).

Where coincidence
intends no harm
who will sue the
first stone in
celebrating?

Thanksgiving Day
1967

L. Z.

LITTLE

When Little Baron Snorck was born into universal society (only about six thousand years old) his first cries were music. But it will be a question until the end of his book and after whether he learned to speak words. The logic of doubt later became very clear to his mother.

He has a lovely head (the windfall of a caesarian) Madame Verchadet von Chulnt, his mother said.

His father, Dala Baballo von Chulnt, immediately saw Baron as a dolphin. The curve made by his nightgown as his chest rose above the sheet of his crib positively soared as over the first chaos of sea.

It was Christmas and something should be said about his family that had come to greet Little Baron.

As Dala Baballo found no time to see family there is no need to describe them individually. They always arranged to meet in town to assure their arrival together and were in a sense one person—that is the Contessa Murda-Wonda, Dala Baballo's sister, who for all her stature depended on the family's attentions. She never had enough of them and would never have had enough had the family been twice its size and many times as compassionate. She suffered. She suffered at births, christenings, confirmations, receptions, weddings, at all happy occasions, remembering things—for no one remembered as well as she. And when she remembered she took on the centrifugal power of a revolving-armed Hindu goddess of the fierce type running her faithful down as an act of love.

Verchadet's family loved more elegantly. They had accepted Western ways. Medicine had made them mild. They exchanged sedatives, vitamins, and antibiotics—in time of great need, aureomycin—and on happy occasions such as this Christmas eve, mild capsules for digestion no more harmful than lozenges.

Verchadet's mother, Tearilee, "believed," and had hazel eyes which disarmed Dala Baballo, indifferent himself to belief, and his sister Contessa Murda-Wonda, not so indifferent, with the tearful piety of their look. Delicately with an expiating lozenge in her mouth Tearilee was trying to convince them, not overtly at the moment, how happy little Snorck would be if brought up in the faith.

"Don't you feel better already, mama," her eldest daughter interrupted. This was Lucy Drishchay all of ninety pounds of model and well-being, continuing her disquisition on the efficacies of the lozenge she had just given her mother. Hiram Drishchay, her husband, noticed politely that "mother" had not swallowed it yet. "But Hiram," cried Lucy, "you don't need to swallow it—it works instantly." Tearilee hurried to assure them—"Bless you, it has opened my eyes."

Mr and Mrs Esfelt, Tearilee's youngest daughter and son-in-law, sighed heavily, judging Verchadet's ash trays as they looked for a cigarette. Not finding one, Esfelt turned to Lucy, "May I have one of those lozenges. We had an early lunch."

Uncontrollable cries came from Little Baron's room. "I wish I could give him some of this candy," mumbled Mrs Esfelt after she had ravished a huge bonbon herself.

But it took Verchadet six months to find out that Little Baron, still toothless, would be quiet only when he was soaking thru a crust of bread as she played him his music box.

c c g g
a a g
f f e e
d d c
right to the window
left to the door
up to the ceiling
down to the floor

Dala Baballo's expressively long arms were tired. Had his spirit the biceps of a baboon and the zeal of a Turk praying to Allah the flesh would still be weak. He could not bounce his son up and down again. He had counted twenty while singing Mozart's jingle to the words already given here, and as if rocked by a boat he set his son down in bed —still pleading "more, more"—amidst his set of rhythm band instruments.

"My ear drums," he said with casual sickishness to Verchadet who had come into the nursery.

"I know," Verchadet sympathized, "but they can't always be tuned to your projected works."

Baballo had been put into his place, that is into his own mind, again. After all he thought: poems come as you live them. Life's long, time fleeting, lovers bleating lovers greeting, endure.

3

"It's time to go to sleep, Snorckie," said Verchadet.

"No," said Little Baron, ringing his triangle. "Baballo, I wrote a composition. Like Mozart! You think only you're a great artist, you're a jealous pig."

"Yes? How's the piano?"

"No good! I know 41, let me see, 51, no 61 songs," Snorckie added rapidly as he clashed his cymbals. "Dalo, is Mozart dead? What's dead?"

"W-e-ell, never mind."

"What do dead people do?"

"Nothing, they sleep."

"Where?"

"Under flowers."

"Does everybody have to die?"

"Not really."

Little Baron looked serious and tearful. "I don't want to die and I most certainly don't want to sleep. Is Mozart dead?"

"Not really, if you play his music he's alive."

"Then composers don't die?"

"And—poets don't either."

"You mean the man who wrote *right to the window, down to the floor* too?"

"Maybe."

"Why maybe? You know, Dala, we picked a good profession," said Snorck kindly as he dozed off to sleep.

3

The porch of the music school Little Baron went to had slender pilasters ordered from Europe that stood right in the center of the city. The lobby inside was dimly lighted like a theatre when the curtain is about to go up. On its pseudo-Tudor walls hung old instruments, programs advertising concerts of the season as well as seasons gone by, and an illuminated testimonial hung by a golden braid from an hautboy—this in honor of the old director who had once played music. All his friends, and he had many, had signed the testimonial, and since they never died they swarmed continuously. The director himself walked thru them as tho his violin cushion were tucked under his chin.

Verchadet and Little Baron went there twice a week. She was not vain, and no one knew that Little Baron could play "41, 51, no 71 songs and the Star Spangled Banner" —as he told everybody who came to his house and was an excuse for staying up late—on the piano. He had started at three and was constantly swelling his repertoire. Now he was four.

But Mrs Runnymeade whose class Little Baron attended did not know this. She had a bit of a moustache and was as gentle and as accentual and as round as old Vienna. As much as he spoke at home, he never spoke in class—not a syllable!

"What did they do in class?" Verchadet, itching to know, asked him.

"Nothing!"

"You mean nothing?"

"Nothing!"

"Then what did they do after that?"

"Nothing!"

"Nothing?"

"I won't say something when they did nothing!"

"Did anyone sing or play?"

"A boy."

"Can he play?"

"No!"

"What's his name?"

"Stewie."

"Why don't *you* play sometime?"

"Because they don't know how to and I won't tell them!"

Several weeks later Mrs Runnymeade was confiding to Verchadet.

"And you know, he clutched the little violin and wouldn't let anyone get near it. That's the first time he has participated with the others, tho he still hasn't said a word. And what's more wonderful, he played the piano," said Mrs Runnymeade, pronouncing the last word with such tenderness she smiled all over her moustache. "Mind you, at least a score of songs and the Star Bangled Spanner—of course I mean the Star Spangled Banner—to which we all stood up and sang. I don't know that he approves of our singing because he turned around and scowled," she said with a titter. "And you should see him hold that violin. I must speak to the director because he's much more advanced than the other children and is ready for individual instruction. Won't you come in now because he doesn't seem to want to let go of the little fiddle."

Back turned on the world, on home, on plaudits, on praise, Little Baron, leaning his forehead on the curved portion of a grand piano, choked the fingerboard of a quarter-size violin.

"No!" he shouted as Verchadet came into the room.

"Little Baron," said Verchadet.

"No!"

"Little Baron," said Verchadet. "It's the only one the school has. You may play it here sometime when you can."

"Leopold Mozart wouldn't have said that to Wolfgang Amadeus," he replied bitterly.

"Well you can't play it, can you?" smiled Verchadet.

"I can so," he said tucking the chin rest in place and assuming the stance of the director of the school.

After a few fierce open strings followed

```
c c g g
a a g
f f e e
d d c
```

"Why you don't say!" said Mrs Runnymeade.

"Why not," said Little Baron. "What did Nicolo Paganini do when three strings of his violin broke? He played on the fourth. Which was the fourth?" he asked his mother.

Verchadet anticipating what Snorckie's second display of "reading" within a minute or so of the first might bring on was, she thought it over later to herself as always, perhaps too soon embarrassed. Unlike all mothers, for she talked to very few, she had never read *What Mother Should Know For Peter—Aged 4*, nor the rest of the series, *Aged 5*, *Aged 6*, and *Pre-Youth*.

Shortly before Little Baron was born she was so disconcerted by him she decided on a pediatrician who poohpoohed the word *psychology*. At that time also she composed an opera that Baballo thought would surely mean an honorary membership in the Club of Music Composers. "I'm not interested," she told him. "When I'm preoccupied I don't think, and I wish everybody were like me." Verchadet, who did not mind learning tempered by politeness, did not at all mind Little Baron's saying to her that he knew three Henry's—Henry Adams, Henry James and Henry Filler—a neighbor's little boy, provided Little Baron had enough manners not to bother the wide world with over-heard confidences of Baballo's midnight preoccupations.

Otherwise a nice person, Verchadet was occasionally obstinate to the point of refusing to read—considering she was a mother and that reading all the time in constant reminder of being a mother is the least there is to it.

In short, since her day meant only cleaning a three story house, making the beds, answering the telephone, adjusting the thermostat for the hot water, setting out Baballo's breakfast and aspirin, ironing his shirt collar so *"that at least"* (his words) would be without a crease, again sweeping out the fuzz from the blankets which Little Baron had dragged behind him into the hall while imitating Carmen clicking her castanets, and by this time of day getting home to set out the dinner service—Verchadet was afraid that Little Baron might delay her by telling Mrs. Runnymeade all of The Life and Four Tunes (as Little Baron insisted the title should read) of Nicolo Paganini by—she didn't have time to remember—and illustrated in color. For Little Baron remembered all the words of every book Baballo and she read to him, provided he heard them right the first time. If he didn't, no amount of pointing out his error would convince him that he was wrong. She was not at all surprised a year later when he remembered all of Bach's Third Partita after he had hurried thru it a few times as he said at "brake-no speed." With notes it was different, but with words—"it is just too bad about you, Verchadet, you're wrong, why," he would insist, "I'm are (I am, Verchadet would correct him) I'm are," he would say, "saying it right." And remembering a wisp of comment Baballo on one occasion permitted himself, he would add: "Musicians are noteworthy—eh, mummie?"

In short, Verchadet afraid she might be delayed said, "Little Baron, Mrs Runnymeade isn't interested."

Since Little Baron could be moved by the tones of

voices and hints he put his thumb in his mouth—he always did when innate goodness placated his temper—, laid the unwanted violin on the piano stool, and turning his back on his teacher walked out of the room.

"We'll air you," said Verchadet in her most highhanded manner to Snorckie. He walked on beside her still with his thumb in his mouth.

"Mummy," he said, beginning tentatively to remove it as they came to the park some streets away from the school.

"In the Egyptian wing of the museum. You've seen him before," she said, as she noticed a troop of young men wheeling baby carriages—actively participating in planned parenthood.

"I'm sorry," said Snorckie, finally taking his thumb out of his mouth.

"What good does that do?" she said somewhat relieved.

"That's the surprise," said Snorckie talkative again. "We'll surprise Dalo." (Whenever Little Baron's thought took a crucial turn it played a variation on his father's name, as the reader may have noticed.)

"Verchadet, does the poet-professor, you know whom I mean, Lada Dala, make as much money as Einstein? I know—*because* Baballo told me Einstein is a science-t," here Snorck stressed the last letter, "and knows all about the stars and what's more plays the violin."

Before Dala became a "poet-professor" he had lost his source of income. Snorckie's most unrewarding impression of him was his dropping in for a hurried lunch, burdened with blue exam books from the "institute." But for baronial honor, let it be said that he earned enough to keep the piano in tune.

"Now let's see," said Snorck babbling, "was it the piano tuner or the plasterer whose name was Einstein?"

It was, in fact, the plasterer whose name was Einstein. Listening to Snorckie's repeated playing of a Brahms' Hungarian dance on the phonograph and slapping the hanging ceiling under the attic by way of accompaniment he had stopped to say to Verchadet, "Lady, any child who listens to one record for a whole day will be a great virtuoso."

"The plasterer," Verchadet replied to Snorckie.

"Right," said Snorckie glad that peace was restored. "And do you know what he said?"

"That you would be a great virtuoso."

"That's the surprise, because tho a tuner knows his pitches, he doesn't know what's on my mind as much as the plasterer."

"That's why he's only a plasterer," said Verchadet sadly like a musician.

"That has nothing to do with it," said Little Baron, "because our ceiling is almost as high as the sky and you remember when he was working on it he said, when he was a boy he could play the violin like Einstein—*because* his name is Einstein."

Verchadet was slightly baffled.

"And if Dala, Lada, Dalo Baballo knows what's right" —Snorckie sounded righteous—"and what can make more money for him than a mere tuner, because all a tuner makes is a good accompanist, he would buy me a violin. Why don't we buy it now and surprise him?"

"Why not," said Verchadet thinking how she had stepped thru the hanging ceiling and paid for it.

"Verchadet," said Snorck, "and do you know what our secret is? Beginning tonight we must tell Baballo you're my accompanist and that I'm a violinist."

![6](musical staff with large numeral 6)

"Balo, It's a Stradivarius," said Snorckie forcing his father's nose close to the *f* hole.

"Antonius Stradivarius Cremonensis
Faciebat Anno 1724 "

With unstudied surprise, his left eyeglass lower than his right Baballo read back what he had seen, including his bibliographical note of the trade mark: "within two free-hand concentric circles, a cross over A S." Eyes still unaware that his glasses were not focused, he looked completely credulous at Verchadet as if to ask "at what cost?"

"They all have that," she smiled at him as he still seemed anxious to be gullible.

"They all have that," said Little Baron, "or it wouldn't be a Stradivarius," not realizing that his mother meant it wasn't.

"No, really?" said Baballo to Verchadet feeling the loss of an antique.

"A good buy," he said sadly turning to Snorck, "why the case must be worth—" "Twenty dollars," Verchadet whispered. And as he tapped it he straightened his glasses. He patted Snorckie's shapely head: "Play something!"

"What would you like, Bachmonitor or Johansen-bach?"

"Snorckie, you say Rachmaninoff or Johann Sebastian Bach."

"Not really," said Snorckie.

"As you wish," said Baballo, "a violinist ought to know. Anyway, tonight I'll settle for Bach without Johansen and monitor."

Amidst fierce squeaks Baballo thought he recognized "America."

"That's *My Country*," said Little Baron, not completing the title, in a hurry to get on to his next offering.

"You've an ear, son," said Baballo obviously trying to forget his own. "What about some reading before bed-time?"

"The Illicy," Snorck requested. (Sometimes Baballo read *The Odyssey* and sometimes *The Iliad*.)

"*The Odyssey*, Snorckie."

"The Illicy in English translation."

"Yes, but called *The Odyssey*," said Baballo.

"If you want me to understand, you'd better speak in a different anguish," said Snorckie impatiently.

"A different language," Baballo corrected him.

"All right, a different anguish," Snorck nodded.

For some weeks Dala had been able to shorten the reading sessions by enacting a little scene very familiar but fresh to his son who took part in it. Dala donned a sheet which made him Eurycleia. Holding an imaginary torch, he led Snorckie acting Telemachus, Greek as a drawing of Flaxman, but in shirt and pants, to his bedroom.

At the same time Baballo read Homer: *opened the door of the handsome room and sat down on the bed, and stript off his soft shirt which he gave into the wise old woman's hands. She folded it up and smoothed it out . . .*

"Not there," Snorckie inevitably ordered wherever *there* happened to be, and after some delay Baballo concluded: *hung it on a peg beside the bed-frame and left the room pulling the door.*

"Don't forget the bolt," said Little Baron, after Baballo had purposely tripped on the landing, over the sheet which he had dropped to be picked up later.

"It had to be a violin?" he answered his own question, when Verchadet and he could at last enjoy the blessing of speech.

"I have my own fears," she said, forcing a peg of the violin she was trying to tune. "Don't interrupt me."

Sybil Greate taught Snorckie the names of the strings by colors. She herself was always a smiling brown study, arriving late for the lesson, almost too straight, Verchadet could not help thinking. Miss Greate never brought her own too valuable fiddle. She illustrated on Snorckie's quarter-size:

"Little Baron, my fingers are too thick to hold down the right color," she said.—"I'm not used to your fiddle, but you must get used to it.—I'm surprised, Snorckie, why Snorckie, the red is flat.—Good, good, Little Baron, the blue sounds true.—O the green that's as if it had never been," and she would hurry to strain a peg, ending her sentence a minute later, "tuned."—"O but you must play with expression, dolce, sweetly, dolce that's Eyetalian for sweetly, Snorckie, and the white must be heard very, very bright! Little Baron, will you ask your mother to give me that last note on the piano?"

"What color?" Snorckie questioned.

Verchadet accompanied him in a text of exercises called *Scratch A While*.

Miss Greate also taught Snorckie "the notes."

"Every good virtuoso," she told Snorckie who held his mouth open and Verchadet who watched the half-hour go by on the clock as her left eye—the weaker one—acquired crow's-foot, "studies theory. Now this big round empty thing is a full moon. And if you add a stem to it, it's a half-moon."

"No, Miss Greate, my father who's a Greek—or is he a Turk, Vechadet?—calls that *phi*. That line, let me show you," Snorckie said, applying great effort to Miss Greate's pencil, "goes through the center. Or is it *fee?*" he asked exposing the Greek letter to Verchadet. "Full fathom fi'," mumbled Verchadet.

"No," Miss Greate interrupted him gently, firmly taking the pencil out of his hand, "this is music—it's different. And this with a stem attached to a bright black darkened thing is a quarter-moon!"

"Now don't tell me," Snorckie begged avidly, "don't tell me, Miss Greate, I know, this" he said pointing to a blank space of a staff, "is a new moon."

Remember that Verchadet was only a mother that Little Baron had made his accompanist, and she had never read *Pre-Youth*. All this musical moon kind of teaching was very hard on her. After stretching patience over half a term of lessons, she came home one day and asked Baballo, "what do you teach?" She had never asked him this, so that all he said Hamlet-like, or hammock-like as Snorckie would say who had seen the movie, for Baballo was rocked and racked continuously by passion, was: "Ha?!"

"Is all education today moon and sub-moon?" asked Verchadet.

"Moon Mullens, what do you mean?" said Baballo.

"And the spectrum? What about the spectrum?"

"Are you out of your mind, Verchadet?" he quavered.

"Don't quaver," she said, "my right ear is queasy as it is. All I mean is, I shall soon be as moonstruck and as color mad as the dye industry."

It was St. Valentine's Day and Baballo, who was not

unromantic and sometimes not too slow at understanding Verchadet, said: "Don't be that way Verchadet. Isn't Snorckie learning the fiddle?"

"He is, but not his color exercises. Maybe I'm wrong. With me, you hear him every evening don't you, he's up to Bach's Third Partita, but with Miss Greate he doesn't know green from red."

"Tse-tse-tse-tse," said Baballo, looking like the poet-baron behind the Great Wall of China he felt he was at the moment. "Wait a minute, Verchadet," he said, as he hurried upstairs. A minute later he came down. "Verchadet, St. Valentine's Day—your poem!

> We may be old-fashioned,
> But—we're impassioned.
> When a fiddle string's red
> Music is dead!
> Then up with Johansen
> Bach and his ensign
> Or we'll be singing with colors
> And painting red hollers
> A note is a note
> And comes from the throat!"

"Stop, Baballo," Verchadet said. "That makes sense. I'm too run-down to make Tuesdays at four any more. Snorckie's getting a man teacher!"

8

In the house of Murda-Wonda all spoke at once.

"No let him *play* first, that's what he came for, didn't he? Let him *play* first, then he'll take off his hat and coat."

The vestibule was filled with relations and neighbors. For the first time in his life *Snorckie* was stymied.

"Does he have a good teacher?" Contessa Murda-Wonda asked as Snorckie still wearing his ear muffs opened his violin case.

"A woman," said Verchadet.

"A woman?" queried the Contessa with a profound look and a tone of grief in her voice.

"A woman," called Count Murda-Wonda from his bed in the next room, "no good!"

The Count, the blueblood of the family, unmentioned till now, did not come along with the others to celebrate Little Baron's first day in the world, for a reason that will become apparent soon enough. Years ago—he carried his years like a debutante—Count Murda-Wonda had left his food and chattels abroad and arrived in the States with his title only. Six feet seven inches tall, wiry but not broad, hired by the day—continually threatened with being fired at any time—he had worked up to the position of reception-ist in frock coat decorated with a white carnation at the elegant dress house owned by his nephew, a commoner by birth. Every slack season the nephew unflinchingly approached the Count in an all too familiar attempt to ruffle his composure and asked him to look more dignified so as to avoid offense to absent buyers. Not that the establishment could not have thrived without the commoner—the Count sometimes confided to the shipping clerk, his son, four inches his junior and clearly a less robust replica of himself—because it was an inheritance from the commoner's father who had worked hard and died of heart failure to employ a Count. But Count Murda-Wonda never talked back. Instead he retired to the men's room where he padded his inner soles with lamb's wool carried surreptitiously from the operators' tables, so that he might stand an inch taller in his shoes as he emerged to serve all the more.

His chief task was to insist that his nephew's customers sit. In effect he stood guard over them after they were seated in gilt cane chairs padded with shot velvet which he rushed to them at the door, tho he never appeared rushed but impressively lean from noblesse oblige as he strode toward them thru the reception room. His height convinced them when he insisted: "Sit, it's a treat."

In the twenty years he had worked in the establishment he had himself forgotten the pleasure of sitting. In himself he was the wished-for client of the modern interior decorator to whom the sitting position is unsightly. He never sat in the subways and was at once recognized by conductors, stenographers and messenger boys as an aristocrat.

In forcing his nephew's customers to sit, he was by nature on the side of the gods of health and good breeding. His nobility without forethought caused the commoner nephew—nearly his height and twice his girth—who never cared to do anything but sit, legs wide apart, to puff over twenty feet of reception room from his office to the door where his clients remained fixed till he greeted them.

In the men's room the Count not only grew taller but ate

his lunch, stretched out on a rug which he vacuumed with maternal care for his son who joined him. Count Murda-Wonda ate gingerly because his dental bills were mounting.

After using some dental floss by raising himself on one elbow and staring into the black tile of the side wall, he turned on the other elbow to his son, who looked not at him but up at the coffered ceiling, and invariably said: "Ah, poetry!" He had an extreme fondness for the German language which he had learned as a child, and still felt for as a child:

> Hören sie, sehen sie
> Wissen sie was?
> Kochen sie, picheln sie
> Essen sie das?

And receiving no answer, went on:

> In alten Wald
> In finsteren nacht
> Sitzt einer alter
> Italiener und tracht—

DASH! it was time to get back to his watch.

Leading this hard life all day, it was natural that the Count should immediately take off his frock coat as soon as he came home in the evening. Then his only garb was a deep red pair of pajamas of Canton crepe heavily embroidered with his monogram over the breast pocket—in which he always kept a neatly folded handkerchief of lighter red —and a rampant dragon over the other breast, the end of the dragon's tail writhing somewhere near the Count's solar plexus tied in by a flowing contrasting white sash of satin. He was always lying down, whether eating his meal in stages or receiving neighbors and visitors in a steady stream—smoking constantly and infuriating the Contessa with his gracious request for a sixth glass of tea and another teaspoon please. He slept only four hours a night, some-times even in these hours making the rounds of the rooms of his large apartment—never sitting down, one reason for it perhaps that the comfortable antiques the Contessa had col-lected "were too good," as she said, "to be rubbed out." She often forbade her immediate family to sit in them. It tired her "chasing the dust all day from the furniture." She her-self always ate standing.

Accordingly, everyone had eased over to the Count's bed where the family usually sat in his house. Verchadet had finally persuaded Snorckie to take off his hat, ear muffs and coat. Between obeying others' wishes and mother's Snorckie's first choice was others' tho his actual choice was mother's. With this interlude weathered, Snorckie stood at the heavily valanced foot of the bed playing the Loure from Bach's Third Partita—especially the chords. Intent on showing everybody that music was serious, Snorckie always picked what seemed to him the most difficult piece in his *stu-dium,* as the Count termed it, stressing the German word in a wordly manner.

"SNORCKIEEE!" roared the Count, who had a good heart and had never yet raised a young violinist to the ceil-ing, at the same time that Little Baron executed the last chord with a flourish, "Easy does it!" And while guests and royalty roared "Hurrah! Hurrah! Hurrah!" up went Little Baron in shirt sleeves as Baballo, lost somewhere talking to an old gentleman, his father, would never dare bounce him.

"Please the Count and his money's on the table," shouted the Count back on his bed. "ROULETTE! Ha! Ha! Ha!" The contents of a change purse crashed on the tea-table beside the bed before Snorckie could see how the purse disappeared. "Ha! Ha! Ha!"

"He's a baby," said the Contessa of her husband to Snorckie, showing embarrassment in the presence of her nephew's talent. "Say! what are you so happy about? You'll break my table, Count!"

"Truck on down, Count!" yelled the usually mute but Westernized young Count to his father, as the Count leaped off the bed to comply while the radio played an Armenian folk tune and the family continued talking all at once.

"My rug! Count!" The Contessa keened with despair at the floor.

"Easy does it," the Count outbraved her as he fell back into bed.

"That's where he learns manners," said the Contessa attempting to smile at Snorckie.

"Never mind, my Contessa; Baron, play more, Fantasia Capriccio!"

"No," said Little Baron hurt to the quick, "do you know what I just played?"

"Who wrote it then Piotr Ilytch Leonovitch Stepanovitch Ivanovitch Dimitricki Zhikovski?"

"Bach," said Snorckie with venom.

"Oh Bach, I know him. He was an old friend of mine. For years—"

"No!" said Snorckie, gulled it seemed, somewhat pale with jealousy. "He's dead."

"Dead!" said the Count. "My old neighbor, dead! Who told you? Ah, oh, my old neighbor Bach!"

"Do you know his first name?" asked Snorckie.

"Snorckie, what does it matter? Dead is dead. Play another piece to remember him by. Snorckie, please!"

"What!" said Snorckie, "don't you know enough—that music is music—Brighteyes—you Zeus Cronion—and peace is P-E-A-C-E?"

"Ch . . ch . . ch . . that's the forbidden kind, Baron, Baballo," yelled the Count, "what kind of language are you teaching him? Brighteyes? Zeus Cronion?" Baballo did not seem to be around.

"What do you MEAN?" said Snorckie.

"Leider, leider, Forbidden to Walk on—Defense de, Verboten!" said the Count abstractly.

"You thermo—" Snorckie began tentatively and then snapped out at him, "you thermotitious mouse!"

"And what do you mean?" asked the Count with a slight pause before happily bursting into a wailing song:

"Ah - ah - mouse
In - my - y - house
How - do - you - slee - e - p
Ah - oh - oh - my - shee - p."

And then decisively: "IN ALTEN WALD!" Snorckie clapped his ear muffs on, chortled tearfully, and walked off.

After some time the music was forgotten. Verchadet heard herself talking louder than the rest of the company dawdling around the still bedded Count as they were beginning to leave.

"Verchadet," said Baballo, "don't leave burning cigarettes in ash trays," as the Count nodded gravely to him by way of farewell. The Contessa stood beside her largest wing chair with a look of vague severity, oblivious to Snorckie and the old gentleman sitting in it now that she would be—of all people—alone again.

"Snorckie, come often," said the old gentleman. "Tell Baballo come. Tell you-mama. Come you-self?" he asked kissing Snorckie as he neared the end of English.

Snorckie understood perfectly: "I come ma-self!"

"Good! good!" said his grandpa. "You smart guy!"

"You smart guy!" laughed Snorckie.

As they neared the door, the Count bowed them out somewhere from the top of his six feet seven. And hardly on the other side, Snorckie asked Baballo: "Why, Dala, if everybody loves grandpa are they always telling him what to do?" The answer seemed simpler to Baballo, when, some months later, after being told that his grandpa had died, Snorckie asked tenderly if he might have a real skull and cross-bones for Hallowe'en.

And Baballo wrote his poem

You are old Dr. Gluillens
Your fiddle is bent
Its father was aery
And played it in Ghent

It sang in Cremona
And bōwed where it went
With its strings tied to Florence
He played it in Ghent

Its mother was rosin
And never forlorn
To the bounds of spiccato
The mellow French horn

The ferment of spruces
That flowed thru its wood!
The firkins for juices
Are now gone for good

Sweet gherkins and spices
Were not untoward
Pizzicato, vibrato
Each note was their ward

A mite of St. John's bread
That fiddle of Ghent
With ninety staccatoes
To one bōw it went

But look! the low elders
The hut which is thatched
The sounds by the wellhead
Are taken detached.

What else was there to do?

Snorckie too had felt "detached" (as in Baballo's poem) for almost two weeks with scarlet fever, no better tho sitting up playing the violin in bed. "Let's play st–" *staying down,* Dala was going to say when the compassionate musical von Chulnt in him hiccuped "–even, son."

Little, who heard with at least a *double* sense when he played, took up any chance hint his own way:

> "when I was sick and lay abed
> with none to tell me what to do

—fertherover—

> in winter I get up at night
> and dress by yellow candle-light
> it is very nice to think"

Inextricably Dala felt himself bound, Little's playmate:

> "Great is the sun and wide he goes
> more thick than rain he showers his rays
> and thru the broken edge of tiles
> grasses hide my hiding place
> and winter comes with pinching toes
> the eternal dawn beyond a doubt"

Verchadet looked in on her ninth climb upstairs, a hand shading crow's-foot of her aching eye from the strong sun in the room, to report Tearilee's third telephone call of sympathy within the half-hour this morning. "Still not resting?"—and left.

The game went on thoughtlessly, largely as Little's urge not to stop fiddling:

Lada:	"all grow up as geese and gabies"
Little:	"and turn the turtles off their legs
	fly as thick as driving rain"
Dala:	"and it moves with the moving flame"
Little:	"the red fire paints the empty room
	and flickers on the backs of books
	that crumble in your furnaces"
Dala:	"humming fly and daisy tree
	in the hedges and the whins"
Little:	"water now has turned to stone"
Lada:	"when I was down beside the sea
	a wooden spade they gave to me
	to dig the sandy shore
	my holes were empty like a cup
	in every hole the sea came up
	till it could come no more"
Little:	"where shall we adventure
	today that we're afloat"
Dala:	"a-steering of the boat"
Little:	"to where the grown-up river slips
	and with bell and voice and drum
	cities on the other hum"
Dala:	"waves are on the meadow
	like the waves there are at sea
	the organ with the organ man
	is singing in the rain"
Little:	"it rains on the umbrellas here
	all made of the back-bedroom chairs
	with trees on either hand"
Lada:	"thousands of leaves on a tree"
Little:	"in the sky and the pail by the wall

half full of water and stars
I could not see yourself at all
how great and cool the room"

"Dala, we perfected it."

"Have we?" queried von Chulnt wondering, what.

"Well! If you'd stood still, like a good violinist when he plays in one place and listens to himself and creates, you'd have heard our *you'rephonie,*" said Snorckie for *euphony,* "you'd have *heard* what you-end-or-we did with those so-called child's garden*s* of verses. We were tired of them but still liked them, so we rearranged them—I call that *perfected it.* We've changed not a word: leaving some out you know they sound only more grown-up. Baballo," Little asked very tenderly, knowing very well that Bach had twenty-two children, "how many children" etc "was he patient with them?"

"I should judge he was," answered Dala.

"Dala," Little Baron said, "do you want to hear *something?* It isn't for you to judge. Lada, I like your line, 'To one bōw it went.' *To,* not *on,* that's just right with *ninety* staccatos. Dala—when is Doctor Prunejuice coming? My throat's—bookmatches which got wet—dry again. What's the use of bed?"

"Matchbooks," Dala said softly to correct him.

Doctor Prunejuice, whose real name was Gluillens, had been coming every day without being called to look over Little, for two weeks now faithfully making him his first leisurely visit in the afternoon, after many urgent morning patients. The brisk doctor, years gone from Baltimore, still looked as if he had carried off some of its convict sunlight from the three white steps of stoops lining red brick rows of completely deserted streets. He had himself played the fiddle as a cultured lad, and—psychology's enemy as has been said before the Doctor was—Snorckie's case history was enough to relieve his serious medical diagnosis. For the rest, Dr. Gluillens' pediatrics was simple: prune juice and fresh air. One look at the von Chulnts convinced him his insistence would have to be with them. "The history of medicine in its contention with ignorance was always the story of patient centuries insisting against hiding acid—well, what is life?" But the Doctor liked the almost foreign courtesies of the boy's parents and acted not to notice Verchadet demur as if she was not there—for both she and Balo could endure chill less easily than smoke.

"Fresh air never caused neuralgia or neuritis or a cold." And again he would tell the story of how his half-Welsh granny forgetting him as a baby in his cradle on the back porch overnight (she herself had dozed off after some prune whip and ambrosia by the fire) found him as he woke up before dawn covered with a blanket of snow, but warm as a fresh brewed pot of tea, none the worse. "Or I wouldn't be here," he assured Snorckie.

"Persisting with the fiddle? Good! Wish I were. There's not much you can do with a virus of *this* type anyway—just let it play out." He had been following "the young man's career" out of self-interest from the time of his first examination a month after birth, when he watched the infant follow his finger until the little head turned to make up for the eyes' incapacity to roll on. "There!"—the doggedness of it was the most intelligence he'd ever served at *that* age.

The Doctor stayed on a while after replacing his instruments in his twenty-year-old case. He believed that whatever thoughts he might express as he sat back the few minutes after the all around unconcern on receiving his check most effected his patient's cure. "Why, sir, I see your gift has come."

"Yessir," Snorckie nodded in its direction, "my Brand Mew Fidelity Recorder."

"I finally wrote to the president," Verchadet smiled.

President
Station WAIF

Dear Sir:

You must agree we are both scoundrels—I for allowing my son to appear over your station, you for not keeping your promise to him after three months. But still under five he refuses to take us lightly, noticeably these last two weeks he has been down with scarlet fever. I would rather not say I trust I may hear from you.

Very truly yours,
(Mrs) V. von Chulnt

She did not of course hint to the Doctor at the substance of her letter, which flashed on her mind. The insult of having to write it shamed her less than her feeling that it was her son's lowered resistance, brought on by his video debut, that had caused this illness. How stupid she had been to let him *persist*, as Snorckie worded it, *perfecting* Mozart's minuet from *Don Giovanni* and *Home on the Range* under the hot lights while the director of the half-hour roared "Roll 'em!" Especially after she had learned that Little had been programed with a ventriloquist and a chimpanzee. Why! the chimp had shown more resentment than she had at the commercial intercalating on the same set, some effete youth of thirty or so syncopating his foot on the floor cluttered with cable, as he sponsored his *Tiny Feed* with a lisp she only once made out:

> When the goothe
> ran loothe
> in the kithen
> my baby thaid
> maybe
> we cath him
> with gravy.

"Was it worth it?" smiled the Doctor.

"Not to me," Verchadet agreed as if he had addressed her. "Tuning a fiddle with klieg eyes is a bit worse than pulling nipples over baby bottles."

The Doctor laughed. "When your young man is well, I judge in about two weeks, he should be shanghaied to the country. I would not risk another variety of spring bug growing up for the summer epidemics. Well! I didn't sleep deliciously last night listening to our neighbors' young dog locked up in their apartment while they went off.—Bye!"

"Bye!" Little chuckled.

They found it thru *The Biweekly Literary Emporium.*

Vacation in New England
"Substance and shadow." ANTHOS, five miles
south of Sider, four miles north of Sweetsider. Dining in commons live in your separate cottage.
Quiet guests.

And pretty soon Dala, Verchadet and Little were walking the one road under mostly elms either the five miles
north to Sider, past the Egyptian lotus pond on the estate of
Antonio Viertel Achtel, or past the general store, church
and graveyard the four miles south to Sweetsider.

The separate cottage backed by a knoll of rock in the
trees looked down from across the road on the sunned and
shadowed classic architecture of the several-gabled roof of
the "commons." The exterior of the cottage of heavy boards
hastily put up was still unfinished. Inside, dusty sheet rock,
broken in one wall repaired with a grate of wire, safely
caged Snorckie's first pet: a field mouse.

"A vole," said Dala.

"Jawohl!" said Snorckie.

Dining—three meals—chilled the obviously unmov-
able heads of the quiet guests in the long glass-enclosed
north porch of the main house or commons.

"George Washington, John Adams, John Alden," Little whispered to Verchadet seated next to him, so hushed that Dala facing them and these three personages, all women, at the large table at the far end, could not hear him. Little Baron had looked long but accurately on entering. Now nibbling at a salad of turnips and beets sprigged with parsley he looked only straight ahead at Dala, and did not dare turn his head to see if his mother was smiling down sideways at him for his good manners. The von Chulnts felt too numerous to break the quiet of a first impression that the three distant, immobile personages shared a doubt of a least stretched smile of welcome. Nearer to Dala before him, dressed sprucely in black at his own small table—not a guest but a Sunday visitor they learned a week later—the composer Viertel Achtel ate with relish, looking out occasionally at the shadows of ducks thru the porch's lead-divided panes. By the time the spoonmeat (dessert) was served Snorckie, looking toward the far opposite end of the porch, saw another small table crowded near the entrance, and whispered again almost inaudibly to his mother: "James Madison." *She* greeted them on their way out, adjusting her glasses chiefly toward Little, "My dear, I *am* glad you're here."

After a nod a few paces onward, "James Madison is the Feather'w'st," whispered Little, who by this time had heard something of the Founding Fathers. A retired army nurse she was in her slight arthritic still tall strict figure the most feathery and indeed Federal of the ladies of Anthos. Few years younger than the other ladies—who hardly greeted her—never resentful in her self-reliance, James Madison unobtrusively became the von Chulnts' self-appointed emissary mitigating the natural xenophobia of the others. Her birthplace Lincoln's Springfield, nurse, a world traveller, she could without trying somehow allay the atavistic gooseflesh of most polyglot fathers or mothers and light any little Abdullah, Rabindranath, Iwa, or Abraham with anticipations of Advent, she was so lovingly curious as to their own heathendoms. Only the turncoat impiety of a Christian heathen disturbed her, but of that—unrighteous as she found it—later.

When John Alden fretted, "Why must that child scratch on his awful instrument every morning," James Madison dared the von Chulnts' rock all alone to find out what Snorckie was really at, tho she had no ear herself. And in a day or so John Alden, appropriating the intelligence from her friend Viertel Achtel as *her* scoop, told James: "Mr Achtel says that the boy's Bach is very accomplished." Lately filling her retired life with books, and books about the lives of their authors, James Madison happily chancing on one of Baballo's endeared it as the only poetry that meant anything to her besides "my" Keats. When Little, who unfortunately ran faster than the ducks, horribly scraped his knees her old second lieutenant's first aid kit brought out such stoicism from him she called him major while treating him on her knees. For Verchadet she reserved her consummate praise, "My dear, you are the purest unsentimental mother I have ever met." Thus in her guileless care for the von Chulnts she innocently attracted to them many friends, who years later would loyally travel *to attend* the violinist's recitals in the city.

Cap of a knee
lock of hair
eyes with their pupils
crown of a head

Bridge of the nose
roof of the mouth
nails of the toes

Crook of elbow
shoulder blades
palm of hand
drum of an ear

Calf of a leg
corn of a toe
corn of an ear

Back home polio raged. In the country Dala walked the one road—in his mind. When the three could not walk, or shower in the midday heat on the rock, the turnips and beets grew too fast for the parsley. The Founding Fathers turned into benign Norns brought more adulators. "If only there were a little distance," Verchadet said abstractly, "it would be less wearing and exciting." That day the vole escaped from its rough cage to share Snorckie's bed.

On a southerly walk thru Sweetsider they came upon Archives Lane, where Baballo stopped to look up at a sign —RUSSELL, THROSTLE & THROTTLE LTD, *Realtors.* "But this is expensive property," said Verchadet who had guessed Dala's thought. "Maybe," Little said, "expensive country." "Baronet colonial," Verchadet smiled. "Look at the cow!" said Little. "We sell warm milk," said the farmer who was there, "to those who want it fresh and un-pasteurized."

The Archives with Corinthian columns on the main street, rather highway, its circle with the most famous church steeple in New England after its English counter-part, seen from everywhere, and turning the corner of the lane at the realtors, across from the Archives, two substantial dwellings in baronial good taste opposite the little farm—continuing, country lane past low land and rivulet from larger water four miles off *as the crow flies* they heard say, for an eighth of a mile to the edge of woods: some rods before these tho, a shed for sale with a smaller, closet-like, behind it. They secured the deed for both outright in a transaction the realtors bothered to handle only for the sake of future neighborly courtesy.

Their country home simulated gables, one over each side of the wings of its triptych effect—the doorstep entrance, roofed over, coming out at the most two feet and placed somewhat to the right against the frame of clapboard. Originally this front entrance had been centered. The left wing, as the interior showed, was added after—a bedroom not more than a berth receding less than half the eighteen-foot length of the shed. Fortunately for Little what at once became his room was filled with a rope bed (without mattress) with at its foot a wall table and chair, so that he could bounce from bed and sit on the table by leaping the chair. The living room had no right wing, tho the rain gutter between its two windows on the façade had affected a wing. Wingless the original shed then owned an oversize tinder and coal oven near the back door for warmth, and a Franklin stove for burning refuse for more warmth nearer the front. There were enough windows front, side and back —each with sixteen panes—to make both rooms cheerful with their pre-Revolutionary outlook onto the neighborhood. The story was that a Laplander the one previous resident wintered there, the round well of heavy cemented stones not deep but by reputation sweet perennially drew water when the artesian diggings of the neighbors ran a trickle or froze to nothing. As for fauna and flora, there were all the animals Little might expect in New England, besides a mulberry, without silkworms, and elderberry with tangles of bittersweet. Little said later, the one mistake his parents made was not to live with the shed—content in it and the smaller rear structure hidden by cattails with its private view of three-quarters of an acre mostly in length down the lane; *they just had to plan* tirelessly to make it liveable, while they wished the smaller shed could be made to look illusory.

Six of Baballo's impetuous strides over the planks of the living room to the back door and out, and *there*—as he stood on the cement stoop a few feet to jump down from to ground—was the view he conceived a Turner seascape had perhaps looked to find in a Claude Lorraine landscape.

Verchadet saw, as she said, a lovely landscape. But the consequences of vision turned out the same for both, and for Snorckie a constant actual fiddling unlike the kind he observed in their distraction.

More precisely he overheard as he observed thru the corners of his eyes—"That arrowroot in the rivulet like Viertel Achtel's lotus, Lada, if landscaped could be white."

"I was thinking the same, Verchadet, only I did *not suggest it* to you after yesterday's mishap," he said shyly as if *it* might still be avoided by both.

"I'll do it. Only agree not to help, I can weed around the arrowroot much faster alone. It'll be white and float. No, I haven't a cold. If anything I feel better after yesterday's sprucing up a bit in the cattails. Aren't you happy we're rid of that unsightly fill and rotten log almost breaking them down, and I do know now one can sink in a marsh." She smiled, implying that her new plan for weeding was so much foolishness their similar tastes could not evade.

"No, let me help. But after that we stop." Satisfied, Little executed a picchetato with the words in mind, "not on your life they'll stop."

As their happiness would have it the shed had been electrified for light and telephone. With a few installations its one living room could be divided by a third of a partition into smaller living room with a kitchen and miniature bathroom at the rear, the water from the well electrically pumped running to both. For this renovation they hired help. The mingling professionals at their different tasks could not always it seemed keep them separate, and Little helped by passing Dala's only tools, a saw and clawhammer, heirlooms from his father, among them. Habitually forgetting to bring such tools, if they ever owned them, they often waited their turn. Not to appear embarrassed for their help during these restful interludes the gentle von Chulnts occupied themselves with disposal, carrying the rubbish of the operations along with a late Sunday newspaper a quarter of a mile down their lane to Sweetsider's dump. The realtors had told them it was good for the marsh to be filled there for future building.

By the height of summer, only weeks after Anthos, Verchadet and Dala had transformed their shed and acreage. They had untangled the bittersweet from the elderberry, shut the cover of the gaping seat with its odor of stacked hay in the illusory back shed forever from now on to be opened only for Dala's clawhammer and saw and the new rake and lawnmower safeguarded behind the door with its wooden latch over which the rose brier they trained was allowed to fall casually, sold the Franklin stove and oversize oven and replaced them by an electric heater, boiler, two-plate burner and portable freezer, nailed a trestle table and bench of Baballo's make to the floor at the kitchen window facing the morning sun and woods, curtained the part of the window not hidden by the stall shower of the bathroom on the opposite wall to afford a peek at the mulberry only when standing with one's back to the sliding door that negotiated entrance and exit, regretted they could not bake potato scones as their parents might have done in the oven they had sold, consoled themselves with a harmonium from a hilltown site of an old great battle in the border state reminding Snorckie of its history when Verchadet accompanied his fiddle, assembled Baballo's desk that had arrived as a kit with instructions that frayed him until Verchadet and Little in short order stood it up whole at the two windows of the now impassable but still simulated right wing of the living room, persuaded Little to accept a mattress replacing the odd heap of blankets he had argued were comfort under him, and bought themselves a sofa for two convertible into a bed which opened would protect them from night visitors by making it impossible to open the front door from outside or in. Two small not too reminiscent Windsor chairs, for the harmonium and Lada's desk, were delivered late. The place was now full, tho not over-furnished to their taste. They could sit back anywhere and still see space between things, or look out, or walk the path between front and rear doors to the country around the house. For Snorckie too it was roomy. He could lay his fiddle case on top of the harmonium when he performed formally, or when he practiced with just enough room for his own unimpeded bōwing in his own lane between the windows of the left wing and the side of the rope bed he could keep it on the new azure quilting.

It was during one of these latter choices that he found himself reading his father's notebook—tho Dala could not recall how he had come to leave it despite violinist's prohibitions on Little's bed:

> rabelais $\geqq$ H. *rab*, master, *le(t)z*, jester; *rab lāvī* (Egy. *lawai*) m. lion; or diminutive possessive, *rebele's?*

"Dala," Little called from his room, "take this back e-midget-ly"—the last word enunciated with command and elegance. "If it has anything to do with music, or what is that diminuendo over crescendo before German B? You can't have them together, even if it's you, in one and the same time." Used to reading most symbols musically he summed up his disgust in a query, "What does it *mean?*"

"Sorry, son," said his father who obeyed immediately—he had been looking for his notebook—"I don't know yet." He might never know, and yet the *yet* sounded almost prophetic of incidents that would follow soon, which could if he mused long enough illuminate his arcana.

James Madison was the first to visit the "restored dream cottage," as her enthusiasm expressed it, *the first* to carry the tidings of its improvements and economies to Sweet-sider, Anthos and Sider. Before leaving her trio of dear friends, she christened their place, as they readily let her, *Riding Hood*—omitting the *Little* that she said would be too obvious, and also the *Red* out of respect to her color of Federalism.

"It's my gummamint, too," said Little, and she kissed him on leaving.

While she was not responsible for all the visitors who followed her to *Riding Hood* many came. None arrived walking, all with the speed of a traffic-saving instinct that impelled them to grind their brakes at *Riding Hood* before they drove past it recklessly into the woods. The owner of Anthos, a lady so huge Little could not name her, paid her respects. *Life gives way and our families,* Baballo had been brooding; and the Esfelts, hunting for a vacation home of their own, somehow came upon their sister's dream cottage with greetings from the Drischays touring Lapland and Tearilee and the Count and Contessa more content at home. The young relations did not stay long after a simple snack of imported canned Dutch ham and several frozen deep dish fruit pies, the best and only comestibles for the happy occasion that the general store of Sweetsider and the two-plate burner of the von Chulnts could bring out.

For the constantly surprised three at *Riding Hood* the visits were a kind of fare more quickly absorbed than understood. Interrupted eating an untasted bite of lunch they at once served the unexpected guest or guests all they had hopefully stored in the portable freezer to last them for a week. One afternoon James Madison brought with her from Sider her wise old friend Gwyn Yare, whose memory of youth was one extended eisteddfod. Together they listened to Little's Veracini, Purcell, Mozart, Honegger and Bach—Verchadet constrained to the harmonium for hours, Baballo lurking now and then at the back door open to his Claude Lorraine. When finally the old sage had recollected all his memories and was ready to go, he smiled affectionately at the young mother and said: "I am sure you know, your son doesn't play, God plays thru him." James Madison then whispered a promise of returning with Viertel Achtel.

The plumber, a pious Mr Arrows, who never laid the tiles of a buried cesspool the shortest distance between two points, defensibly on the mechanical principle that would prevent seepage from the waters of a marsh into a cistern, had coffee with the von Chulnts almost every other day. The tank, or cistern as he called it and had told them, was *septic*. He could find no reason for its acting up so often. But he would observe it—that is exhume it each time it failed its purpose—and with time discover why. His faith that the von Chulnts were carrying not only newsprint but every scrap of paper to the town dump was unshakable. For all that the trouble with their—for want of an elegant word—*plumbing* was heartbreaking. As a precautionary measure, horrified by thoughts of admixture in the pipes that should be running to them the pure waters of the well, they were boiling the water from the kitchen tap. It might happen any time of day or night that Verchadet, or Dala, or Little, or all together hearing a by now familiar noise from the general area of the plumbing under the floor beams would pale. Or aroused from sleep, a smiling Little, showing the space of a recently lost baby tooth, often joined them to see *Riding Hood* bidding as it were to sail away. The rise and fall of water from the bathroom onto the kitchen, living room, and front and rear steps was instantaneous and uncontrollable, allowing them only a murmur of a crescendo in unison of the names of a trilogy of Baballo's recension disembodying the pathos, the terror and ineluctable fate of its happening: "Pia Mia, Le Spectre de la Rose, La Forza del Destino."

They were sad enough to want to go to sleep early after one such tiring session—an evening of bailing water for hours, Mr Arrows not in Sweetsider when Dala telephoned. Snorckie disgusted and tucked in, their sofa converted snug against the front door after mutual warnings *not to flush* until Mr Arrows would come tomorrow to observe again. They had turned off the lights, but the darkness sounded a voice: "Anybody in? A friend of Miss Madison, Reverend Loess." He must have seen the lights go out and did not have to ask his question. But a reverend always had the right to call on his flock unannounced, or as the epic poet wrote, *unforewarned*. The von Chulnts were not quick at excuses: "One moment," Verchadet said impulsively and at once regretted admitting they were home. The bedding hidden on Snorckie's table and his door shut, the bed a sofa again cushioned in its corner for the reverend to sit in, and the hosts in housecoat and robe decently long, they let him in after a minute. "Trouble with the lights? *We have* at home; the utilities, a monopoly, are not responsible I'm afraid as they should be." Dala took the reverend's hat and coat-pocket leather notebook and neatly stored these also on Snorckie's table, quickly shutting his son's door which he had barely opened.

"Everything is so spacious in this little room," Reverend Loess said. Regrettably he could not stay. He had heard so much from Miss Madison about their son's precocious talent. Would he play at Sunday vesper service for the community? That was not an easy request to make to Little and expect immediate compliance, but "of course," Verchadet said as Dala nodded.

Reverend Loess' church was not the historic church of Sweetsider, but the one on the road from Anthos—older, at least a hundred years older, the church *du pays* so to speak, architecturally native in the fine craftsmanship of its interior. "One other favor." He had heard so much about Little's mother's talent. "They would want" to inaugurate the new electric organ—he himself had contributed to its purchase, the antique "pumped one" was so old-fashioned, and the community deserved something new. Would she accompany her son at the vesper service—he was not sure how kind the acoustics would be to her son's he assumed small fiddle, or any fiddle for that matter? He did not recall any instrument other than the organ ever playing in the church.

She would, tho she had never played an electric organ. She assumed it might make it easier for one who never played in public except to accompany her son.

"We have so much to look forward to, thank you, thank you," the Reverend Loess rose, and Dala forgetting the reverend's notebook gave him his hat. Handshakes and the front door closed.

Little was awake, opening his bedroom door just enough to startle his father by thrusting the reverend's notebook thru, "Baballo, why this *simonizing?*" Lada Dala, as he felt, was impelled by his son's swiftness to glance at the opened page that read *Sermon Sing,* and to wonder how Little had read that quickly in the dark, and then as to the meaning of the reverend's title page. But he pried no further. The violinist's door was shut, his lights suddenly on.

Staccatos of an unexpected practice crunched above the voice behind the door. "Verchadet! why did you agree for me? I won't, intend to play in any church. I'd as soon—and won't either—play in a *masque* or a *ginagog* than compete with the Bible."

A wistfulness somehow brought on by his son's slight of *The Book,* from which he had read to Little with no motive in mind other than its sense of story, led Dala—hand on the knob of the only bedroom door in his shed—to say almost inaudibly: "Wait until you are older, son, before you decide." Following in an even softer tone: *"Masque? ginagog?"*

"Yes! you weren't made to listen, but I *heard* James Madison and Gwyn Yare jabbering when they left here last week. 'Poor Mr Achtel—where he probably would like to go—to a *masque* or a *ginagog* rather than *their* church with the little steeple when he comes to Sweetsider on Sundays;

or if he didn't have to, as he must, not to *their* church at all, but just next door to it to buy his newspaper like everybody else, from dear Mr Houston the pharmacist.' " (Baballo and Verchadet, who like everybody else bought their Sunday newspaper at Houston's, had of course heard and met the negro druggist both feared and respected by the customary Sweetsider tolerance accorded to descendants in part of historical Southern families.)

"James Madison said, 'It's a pity, *it's a pity,*' she said, 'Mr Achtel *probably* found our congregation more antisemiotic than *their* church' (evidently the one with *the little* steeple topped by a heavy cross, Baballo guessed, vaguely hurt by Snorckie's interpolation of the letter *o* in the word *antisemiotic*).

"Verchadet, all they'll do is jabber when I play, and the *acootsticks* are bad enough without an electric organ drowning me out. And what do you know about electricity to inaugurate it. You did, *you did* want to remove the stuck plug with a nail file, when I shrieked, *Watch out*, STOP, NO!"

Baballo had his mouth slightly open to speak. But Verchadet, knowing storms pass, merely signed with her left index finger on her lips *say nothing*, turned off the lights of the living room, and the lights of Little's bedroom followed suit in a lightning flash.

11

Vesper adest. Venus starred an autumn sunset over dense gold leaves, James Madison held her arm in Dala's to be safe over the gravel walk of the churchyard. Several paces forward on the evening's cropped grass Gwyn Yare saw the church doors as the "gates" of the 24th Psalm, and Dala moved to compassion by the wide back span of the old man's uplifted head longed to master more than a little Welsh—thinking: if only he could render its sounds in English that made sense, and repay and delight his friend with loyalty in kind.

Verchadet and Little had been alone in the church some hours early for a last test of acoustics—mostly a rehearsal of passages the church walls seemed not to favor. Snorckie could see that she feared, as he tested a small platform under the pulpit for the creak of his new shoes. She had been playing the new organ by herself for a week, and was reluctantly admitting that its effect was not manual.

Soon they would be performing when she would be unable to hear, as now in the empty church she still could from up the nave to her gallery—where electricity seemed to overcome the effort to resist it and hear herself—to hear if they were together.

Little shouted to her: "Don't worry!"

"I'm worried," sounded the respond.

The church filled quickly. As Dala preceded James Madison in her pew to make her comfortable and sit at her right he felt her elbow wrestle. She stammered a name, something like *Th'Fallens.* "Why is she here," she said under her breath, "she never comes to church." "Th'?" Dala queried. There was one empty seat at his right that distracted him. "Oh—" James Madison struggled to breathe, "th'Jezebel—Baal! I've heard her blaspheme at Anthos. Years ago they say she danced ballet in Paris." Dala uncomfortably suspected that James Madison's voice was heard over their row of seats. Looking up he was abruptly aware of staring into the right aisle.

"O she mustn't, she mustn't," Miss Madison whimpered.

He saw a frail lady uppermost in mauve gauze, head wobbling at first, cheeks rouged into two small suns that with the frenzied decisiveness of a pinwheel on its stick whirred quickly past three oblivious parishioners to the seat beside him. Polite he stood up, she was nearly as tall as he. She spoke sympathetically to be overheard as at a performance, "I hope you don't mind." He could only shake his head from side to side, meaning he didn't as they sat down together. And at that moment like the prelate in a painting of her time called "Temptation" his listless smile might have incurred the wayward thought of a resilience which persists in the calves of an aging danseuse who once wished she were thinner. She spoke freely to him, introducing herself as Dea Falin: "They *all* look dead!" His smile did not change. She must have seen or been drawn to James Madison, coming down the aisle. She hovered on her seat— butterfly over a flower. Contrition held the priest of "Temptation" who now turned his head to his left. Were these tears or fears in Miss Madison's eyes behind the thick lenses? The reflections multiplied into a monster moth humming at a window lighted in the night.

Fortunately a brief prayer, a quick offeratory, then

after the *servitude* (as Little later expressed it) the Reverend Loess thanked the community for their share in the organ and the player in the gallery, and with humility and the charity of a great discovery introduced the soloist.

"Lovely," Dea said, then hissed like a fallen angel: "Snakes and pigs, what do they know of the trials of a child of genius, not able to smell out truths from incense."

"So you're the father?" a gentleman sitting next to Gwyn Yare in the row immediately in front partly turned his head to ask Baballo. The father lowered his long, upcurled eyelashes, long a nuisance tangling in the frames of his glasses, as his reply in church. He looked helplessly towards James Madison, but her rapt face, the good angel's, was prepared to listen without the sensuous ear. Tomorrow she would remember to tell Verchadet, "When he plays something happens to his face that's good."

No one heard the organ inaugurated. As Verchadet confided to Dala after, she dispensed with the diapason with all her strength while the voix céleste was deafening her, and only some inbuilt motherly metronome assured her that she and Little were together. Handel's *Largo* transposed for the violin ascended and was greeted with a jungle of applause.

"Never, never, for shame, shame, in church, in church one never applauds—in church," Dala heard James Madison's outraged, tearful voice—feeling every drop, drop of blood of her piety. "Heathens, heathens," she sobbed. He had not applauded, nor had Viertel Achtel next to Miss Madison tho his suspended hands were ready.

Laughing outright at the *faux pas*, as the nymph might in her wild head in the dance of her youth, "Good for *them*, they're alive," Dea countered the good angel across Lada's neutral body. The applause followed each offering of the violinist. Lada heard neither Verchadet nor Little. The contention was too great. The prelate of "Temptation," the good angel sobbing in his left ear and the fallen angel jeering in his right, by the dormant miracle of his philosophy of history that creates backward as well as forward, had metamorphosed into Janus, but not for long. He found himself thinking: "Loneliness is the same everywhere, no matter whom you love." And that was enough to release the bard so that in his grey matter his little Welsh flowed with the song of Llywarch Hen's son from the *Black Book of Carmarthen:*

> O T'd aerie too hid *his* Strad
> dear is 'nt rue cade weary cad
> m' need awe ah gnaw nim(bl') gad

"Sick transit, home again," Little thought and muttered, back in the city, running upstairs to renew acquaintance with his room. It was the largest in their brownstone, with sunny windows nine feet high, and would be his music studio in the mornings and his study in the afternoons. To their surprise Baballo and Verchadet had easily arranged for Snorckie's schooling at home, under their own tutelage. Perhaps the district school superintendent was impressed that a boy, hurrying towards his sixth birthday, knew the difference between an inflected and an uninflected language, and that Verchadet who would be teaching him Hebrew, Greek, Latin, Italian, French and German had kept equal pace. Perhaps Baballo's rank as professor was warranty for his modest somewhat altered outline of trivium and quadrivium that would take care of his son's delectation for the next four years. One of the few apolitical gentlemen, strangely with some authority in the school system, the superintendent was amenable to Little Baron's polite request for "permission" to sort thru various books and documents on the shelves and desk in the office where his parents to begin with timorous soon discussed their own fitness with ease. Little's several interruptions with questions he immediately answered himself were finally rewarded with the superintendent's consent. "Well," he smiled, "I can hazard one experiment in our great city. Little has been a graduate of the Montessori method for almost three years. I was, I may tell you now, in the audience at the *District Schools Festival* last spring, and your son's *Gavotte* stopped one of the older boys in the middle of at least one profanity. Besides you assure me, Little is registered in an accredited music school. He will not be running wild playing his fiddle."

Gaelic *run, rune = beloved* or *mystery*, Dala meditated listlessly as he stepped across the threshold of the superintendent's office.

Whatever the solicitous graces sometimes awkward or unexpected of the world, Verchadet was looking forward to the repose of routine at home. She preferred her chores to the graces. The violinist preferred Venetians to shut out the excessive sunlight in his room. "All musicians work best in the dark." To his simmer of protest she responded that she might, like Baballo, profess to go to work elsewhere. Little compromised with unforeseen virtuoso affection: "No, Verchadet, you need me to wash the rosin off my fingers." She then took some cloth a yard wide, cut it in half down its length, to make drapes for the pilasters of the corner windows so as to trap the sun's glare where it shone in strongest, and Baballo hung them from their dizzy height as soon as he returned from the first day of his new term at the institute. When Little saw them descend gracefully to the floor, "That," he said, "is dignified, enough."

The three hours (limited to) morning practice, not without its ten minute recesses every hour, *synched* with the light of the world on week days. His liking for darkness become a side issue, the violinist for years delighted in the curtainless windows—the object of his own wish as it were —as playing his fiddle he ran to stand to the roulade of *The Upanishads*, that is the uniformed sanitation men emptying the barrels of garbage down the street. Verchadet, as Little readily acknowledged, was first to call them *The Upani-*

shads. She was not sure why, except maybe for their lordly uplift in pursuing the discards and a rattling of the brain that went with their work mixed with a sense of purity.

All three von Chulnts received letters a week or so (weeks passed so fast) after returning from Sweetsider—codas as it were to their summer—Little naturally had run to pick up from the postman. They read these silently together as a trio, tho sometimes one or another lagged as their heads bent over them, and unavoidably breathed into one another's ears.

Snorckie's letter was from his friend Curt Budder, dated June, and it read:

> dear friend You played the violin terrifick.
> You will grow up to be a very famous man.
> Your friend,
> Curt Budder
> (Mrs. Doody class 4–1)

It was illustrated with a line drawing in pencil and brown crayon of the performer, head of a mixed breed between child and rabbit in profile, body committed to the *law of Egyptian frontality*, one extended hand alone holding the fingerboard rather like the handle of a shovel whose f-holed scoop formed the belly of the largest imaginable viol, all in plan and supporting the violinist as might a perfectly horizontal strut. Little remembered his June triumph, and the "pledgeum allegiance," and as he thought then he heard "and now good-bye," and how the principal had put her arm on his shoulder and he had placed his on hers. "That was when I wore my King of Music hat," he said modestly, "March, then June, and then Octember. What month is it, Verchadet?"

The letter addressed to Professor Dala von Chulnt read:

> Dear Madam:
> Your place in the scientific world is such that membership in The Natural Institute must appeal to you for several reasons . . .

These followed for two pages, including a table of various ranks and respective fees.

James Madison's letter, addressed to Verchadet, read:

My dears,

I miss you. So does everyone here, as you see from this clipping—I'm keeping on second thought but—from *The Sider Recorder:* "Professor and Mrs. Dale van Chant have gone back to the city where their many winter engagements call, but are expected back at their Sweetsider home next summer. Sider remembers their precocious son Little's concert in Sider church at the vesper service that inaugurated the new electric organ so beautifully played by his talented mother; the applause that followed and the presentation of a red leather scrap book by the Reverend Loess to the virtuoso participant in which he now keeps his press releases. We are sure this one joins them."

I am sorry Gale Bright, who edits the *society notes,* misspelled your name. I phoned to tell her that, and she promises to correct the error the next time. But she did have the good sense to print Little's photo which I took before he went off to church that day. You'll recall it, white shirt open at the collar, rolled up sleeves giving room to his bow arm, as you persuaded him—and as you know it turned out to be warm—and navy corduroys with elastic waist. So sweet. Only I hope he chooses Army instead of Navy when he is ready for it.

One sad bit of news. I just heard that your tool shed was overturned in the Hallowe'en pranks of last night. Not all boys are so considerate of other's possessions as Little is. Don't please let this incident worry you. I am sure the shed can be righted.

Ever yours,
James

Little noticed Verchadet's and Dala's faces as they read the sentences including the words *Army* and *shed.* "Well, if you want letters and friends," he said righteously, "you better not wince, *camel-ionic*—o you know what I mean!"

They did, and decided right then and there, without telling him, to visit Sweetsider briefly in the spring to sell the dream cottage, tho James Madison could see them then only in the city. Nor could Dala ever explain to her what the sigh of his haiku meant.

Ah-me No

Smell of
stacked hay
overturned shed

Little, who by this time kept a "dairy" to rival his father's notebook, did not answer his classmate's letter. His young years arced to his later, as the poet would say: later, he would never flash sentiment, never answer letters after giving up his diaries for only necessary appointment books. But now he still pressed down and flourished his pen in his "dairy":

Anent (*anant?* asked Verchadet, who said *use your dictionary*) Budder—good man all covered with shnow and icy schlush underfoot last winter, when Boomerang the duck bogged in the lake won't leave the floes nor eat and died. Sad thinking of it. And Wednesday is a holiday.

For once, uncertain that the letter addressed to him was meant for him, Baballo was finally saddened into indifference to life, the pursuit, let alone liberties, and did *not* answer it. But still somewhat free from the priorities of professor's blue books he took advantage of the holiday to write

Four Related Unrelated Notes

As soon as my title *professor* spread—someone had read my mail—we became the most sought-after people. But I must sublime all ethics into strict geometry—like the *blessed philosopher* whom I call that, I admit, only to salve my own balm. *Blessed,* he saves me the trouble: "This modification of the mind or admiration of a thing is called, if it happens in the mind alone, wonder (*admiratio*); but if stirred up by an object we fear, it is named consternation (*consternatio*): for wonderment at an evil holds man suspended while regarding it, so that he cannot think of other things to free himself, etc. Ethics III, prop. LII

But when I look into the future, an age of space and rockets when even an innocent fiddler's stance may well have to be astro-nautical and political, i.e. for managerial involvement—cool for profits and intrigues of cultural exchanges between enemy states—then will all art whine, croon, yelp from its invisible floor—

A poet, a lost friend once said, they remembered the past of what had survived, but not the future of what had perished.

How welsh Llywarch Hen's *Lament?*

> Alive 'n' I'll my lamb wed
> neat eyed in debt weed dear head
> a mare wee odd no' butt ah mean head

Verchadet, who almost never wrote letters, intended to answer James Madison's to "my dears," while she waited for Snorckie taking his first lesson of the new term at his music school. She was prevented by conversation, chiefly that of another young violinist's mother she had met the year before, as she noticed shyly that the lady had changed her pendent summer cross for another more harmonious with her fall costume.

13

With every new teacher a violinist starts all over—or from the beginning with *scales*, Verchadet was learning. *Nota bene*, Baballo jotted, *and not until he is on his own does he begin: then*, his pen hurried, *extempore*, as he glanced up at Verchadet, *the note that ends well is blessed.*

The old director of the music school, a continuum of the European conservatory, where Little apparently now also officiated, had heard his American boy draw one note from an open string, at the opening of the new term, and immortalized it with the abiding music sounded off the great foreign names on his own illuminated testimonial hung by gold braid from the antique hautboy. When Little ran down the marble stairs ahead of him, the director oblivious that he spoke to Verchadet (or, as happened rarely, to Baballo) would nod: "You should meet that boy—a genius," he doted. Perhaps the director was mistaking the parents for members of his staff. Miss Sybil Greate was no longer there, having left by default of her one open note she had never exemplified on her own fiddle by not bringing it with her to the lessons.

"Sorry to disturb—Little, Signore Agire Onesto Proba, your new teacher," the director said, as Snorckie was crossing strings in *the* Chaconne, and left as has been said pages back with his mental violin cushion tucked under his chin.

Little pressed his own chin by way of greeting and courtesy, but did not stop crossing strings. The slight, thoughtful-looking Italian had brought his fiddle. Yet without taking it out of its case he already stood in one place crossing strings with empty arms completely absorbed by, as the Swan of Avon termed it, *the ground*. Little's stray glances from his violin bridge obviously endeared him. From now on it was only a matter of who could cross strings faster. They stopped together.

"—da Torino."

"Sì, Turin," said Little whose Italian had somehow advanced.

Signore Proba was the (Scriptural) *type* of Dala's look into the future: the displaced violinist of a late war that left him all the world except his own country to play in, the cultural exchange of concerted enterprise between two erstwhile enemy states. He had come to the States on a temporary visa with *much* hope that the old director's *inflúence* would make it permanent. He spoke, for most purposes, all languages and so spoke none, dreaming his wife might join him some day, *when he had fortune*. If grammar were a test, he was these days forgetting his Italian.

"La mia moglie—weefè—miss—how you say—mi?" he confided to Dala and Verchadet when he met them together. But while the ninety-day visa held, Little, as his aunt the Contessa Murda-Wonda worded it, "was proud of his man teacher." Proba exemplified on his own fiddle, pupil rivalled the sound of the full size, both amplified by duos and a constant run of verbal *espressivo:* "How? Bōw —like how? I'm—*hic opus, hic labor est. Jam post bellum.* Oedipe—you know storia—old member quatuor walk on one (pronounced *wan*) leg. You young, two arms, ten fingers, two legs. Posizione, sta, great virtuoso." (Aside to Verchadet and Baballo: "No, no? you *no* American?") They and Little in unison, "But of course we are, what else?"

Proba: "Maybe, no?" then back to Little—) "Play premier, third exercise Svecik. Bis, more once. Probier. *Moment* (pronounced as in French, probably to mean *momentum.*) Più ah più, *ma*! side of hair—happily!" And the day the visa expired, he was to sail home the next day no polygamist, the conversation took a wistful turn. His eyes shone with a tear or two held back in them saying his good-bye to Little: "Very elegant suit. How much suit? Ever, always *moment* (still as in French) arivederci," as he bōwed out of the room, still crossing imaginary strings of Bach's *Chaconne* as when he first walked into it.

"Scales all over," Little complained a week later.

His second man teacher was Mr Athens Olympus—by his changeful face a gamin hieratic type or a late Greek deity of Marseilles—youthfully approaching forty-five, reputed soloist constantly on tour with his fiddle. When he had time to sit on his European acclaim he could be friendly in conversation and pert.

He reminisced on St. Petersburg nights, "ah those and the Paris Conservatory's," his "triumphal tour of two years ago with his *crossbow*" (as Snorckie enthralled decided he heard it) and his "great friend" the harpsichordist Rutar Neitsnebur, Bearlean, Warshawa, Prague, Vienna, Buda, Pest ("or as their citizenry feel," he remarked knowledgeably, "vice versa")—and the farewell night on the Acropolis: tho, as she nodded, Verchadet sensed something about him less European than not un-American, not mercenary but subject to checks and balances. She was almost sure she had guessed right when he did not show up for half the lessons the first month, and when he did he had to leave early with apologies and a "rain check for the short hour." She verified her guess that he was not willfully dishonest. Soon after (forsaking scales) he and Little had rehearsed Bach's double violin concerto he enthusiastically promised they would play it together at the next School Anniversary Concert—remarking shyly: "My D.A.R. wife and our five little daughters all of whom play instruments will be there with contingent."

"Pensive man, Athens, after all," Verchadet said to Dala, while Little thumped his back with felicitations on his own good news, "I was wondering why at this point of his career he wanted to teach, I had supposed to perpetuate his method, but it turns out, tho his wife is rich as I suspect, he still can't responsibly fall back on Bach alone for his future."

"I'm glad," said Baballo to Little, only to ask him and Verchadet some moments later, what was it they told him on coming home while he was writing. He left his notebook open on a table for them to read, but Verchadet had expected him to listen and was in no hurry to, and Little, too intent on perfecting his part in the double concerto at once, just glanced and would not even ply him with a question about "such nonsense":

> what's the
> future of
> the future of
>
> Chinese
> rabbit hutch
> of Demeter
>
> o my girly whirl
> not another little girl
> any
> little boy would
> give
> equivalent joy

"Honest enough," Baballo said recollectively a day or so later, "and modest too," Verchadet added, "for an Olympian. I've heard Viertel Achtel, who follows reputations, say that Europe's taste prefers Athens' passion to Ztephiah's cold accuracy. I don't, but—." (The great

Ztephiah older than Athens, but from the same East European province, was by now a naturalized American for some twenty years, whereas Athens had just recently filed for his first papers.) "Each genius to his own talents," Verchadet went on, "and if Little ever decides against the violin and for the life of a happy Upanishad let the street-cleaning be honest it's all right with me. I'm not as you know sold to lessons forever." Once Verchadet sheltered the faint shadow of a doubt she held on to it for integrity, unlike Baballo who was always composed to let the sun dissipate the shadow.

The very next lesson, or the one after, Athens remarked casually enough to Verchadet: "I have never taught before, and Little presents a problem. I'm not sure that I have anything to say that would improve his part, for example, in the Double Concerto. I have played it many times and I know of no one who plays it better than Little." Verchadet might have been inclined to agree, but for that very reason Athens' praise of Little's playing impressed her as improbable. Had his D.A.R. wife influenced his opinion? Reasons of propriety? that his prestige might suffer in a joint recital with so young a pupil? Motherly reasons of five little daughters with ten eyes looking into the future of one potential fiddler?

"Already?" Dala said mystified, when Verchadet more or less put her thoughts to him after Snorckie had gone to bed. "Much as I hate psychology," she replied. "Fertherover, as your Chaucer and Little say, I don't like Athens poking the tip of his bow at Little's navel, European fashion. Little has a way of poking back that risks mayhem." "Ah, Verchadet," Dala sighed mostly to calm her worries, not needing to tell her she roused his: "Maybe all that Athens means by no one plays the concerto better than Little is that what comes naturally to the young is at best later only excavated by life—the bloom of a thought, not the bloom which is never dug up. Or are you a philosopher? You say no, and I hope not," he speculated as she often said to him, "beautifully to no purpose." "I can imagine, as James Madison might, an aide to a brass hat or electioneer toad surveying Little's vita at 21 and asking: 'Sir, you're 21 and have worked 17 years, impossible!' And should Little explain, why yes I've been a violinist 17 years, the response might be, 'boy, you're joking, does it take that long?' But you see," Dala went on generously, "Athens is as they say a patrician among performers and all his regard for Little means is: Youth performs if he has it, age drudges."

Slamming the door one evening on returning from another short lesson, Snorckie confronted an anxious Baballo behind the entrance to his brownstone: "To make a short story long, he's not playing!"

"Who's not?"

"O*whim*pus," Snorckie scoffed, "has to *tour* in Curaçao the night of the School Anniversary Concert," and gave way to a profanity.

"Ah," Baballo said, "I'm glad you know where to use the word, but just add the suffix *ah*. Sit down, calm down. There's the name, son, of a precious wood in the Scriptures, as Verch will tell you, that avoids dullness by ending in *ah* in the singular and *im* in the plural."

"He said he would," Little rankled, "I'm thru, with *him*." He'd have dragged his part swaying anyway and not played in tune, Little added in his mind naming each note of several foghorns in the harbor that happened to sound then.

"And what's after the shortcomings of the *corpus delicti*?" Baballo questioned Verchadet aside.

"For which you have paid," she muttered in anger.

Their impasse promised not to be funny. But contingency is stochastic as those who think it over say, and happenings have a way of coming together. It happened that Verchadet's mother, Tearilee, on one of her rarer and rarer visits—her lonely arrival occasioned by the fact that the rest of the family was that hour shopping for lustreware—quickened to tears by her middle daughter's impasse asked, "What kind of a life could a fiddle lead to in *any* case?" Her mature dissent gave Verchadet an idea. It happened she knew, Olympus had told her that he had spoken of Little's abilities, apropos of his own fortunes as teacher, to his impresario, Warlock Endor, and who but Warlock knew better the future of violinists? Didn't he invest in them? Her telephone call, tho Verchadet put the question of investment only circularly, brought a ready answer: *He* didn't. But, if as Verchadet directly said, all she expected of Mr Endor was his opinion of her son's talent, his secretary answered, Mr Endor would be glad to arrange for an audition. Verchadet felt gratified when the dignified female voice at the other end completed the conversation, saying she believed Mr Endor was aware of her son's name—would he please bring his scrap book—and confirmed an hour mutually acceptable.

The von Chulnts arrived at the impresario's together. A portly, congenial man greeted the "professor" (*had he guessed right? obviously he had*), the mother and "naturally" the violinist. He heard him—Little illustrating the most impassivity as it produced the most accuracy—and complimented him, impresario to artist.

Then lightly: "And who is your favorite violinist, Little?"

"Ztephiah," the answer flashed lightning.

"I thought so," Warlock laughed most of a breath, "the top of my list, but difficult often in his demands. I hope, Little, you will oblige old Warlock more and demand less when he begs for a favor."

"I hope so," Little almost flattered him as seemed appropriate.

"And what are your plans?" Warlock turned to the parents.

"To let Little do as he pleases," Baballo said as Verchadet glanced at him momentarily so only he was aware that she glared.

"Mr Endor's advice, if I'm right," Verchadet summed it up quickly to silence Baballo, "is for Little to plan towards a solo debut."

"Exactly, there is no question of going on," said Warlock, and turning to Baballo, "he should have at least a Strad to play with."

"But the Gretch sounds—" Dala faltered.

Time hung on for Verchadet as Warlock looked thru Little's scrap book of press releases—Little almost leaning on the impresario and, saving himself embarrassment, rapidly turning pages for him.

"Who is his teacher?" Warlock asked Verchadet.

"Mr Athens Olympus," she said.

"Why, yes," he said, "a great artist—who has gone in for teaching. My personal—merely personal—feeling is the *pro* never has the time away from the concert hall to analyse what he does there so he can best teach it to others. But the great teacher is the best soloist in his studio, and can save the precociously gifted the most regrettable subsequent effort." Baballo and Verchadet were both aware of listening, Baballo somehow unsure that he was not lost along the way.

Little's ostensible future impresario went on: "There is Imam Betur who can execute any difficulty of technique to perfection, he can as his pupils say make wood play. I wish he had been there when I played the fiddle, but he wasn't around then. There is an art of bōwing that makes a *natural* aware of what he is doing every moment of playing so that his elbow never regresses to the rear of the player as it were (literally so to the unaware), but always with a forward momentum—the principle is pivotal. I would suggest you at least allow Professor Betur advise you while Mr Olympus is touring. Genius needs watching," he said to Verchadet. "Well—Little! You must play for me again in six months, and the third time will be in Great Hall."

Thru scales to Parnassus, as Little now translated his Latin: the good-byes were as hopeful as Warlock was comforting. Nothing had been invested, so something was gained. For Verchadet there was no choice. Little would not return to Olympus. She must to Betur, he urged.

Little's third teacher—and last, not counting assistants who taught scales and exercises by which their master weeded or finally took over their best pupils—some never reached him so he was rarely prey to boredom—Little's *best* teacher taught as most people eat: biologically speaking, out of need. Known for the highest fees in the industry, he could forgo fees generously for his final aim: that by watching genius be accomplishèd—the grave accent on *accomplished* not exactly his misplaced foreignism but an example of his messianic dedication. Time was no option: he taught from seven in the morning to eight in the evening, every hour a race that never ran short on the pupil, most often running over, if he ever picked a pupil so unromantically modern to test the teacher by stopwatch. So that Betur's day stopped nearer nine than eight in the evening on most teaching days, in some weeks seven.

He taught all ages. Some he had cradled, and from then on to the middle years, so that genius mounted to deeper genius, and when it flinched it could always return to him even if it had hurt him. And when a composer wanted an unregistered note that no violinist had played before on that instrument of all possibilities, Betur in his leisure found it on a string and found a good scholar to play it, tho he himself could not bear to listen to it.

But Little's story is not a chronicle of teachers. The point of it is Little was the pupil all teachers long for—as Verchadet for all her astuteness had still to find out—and Betur the teacher of fortune.

In character the von Chulnts arrived at Betur's studio together: Dala Baballo mainly to disprove the academic fiction of *the omniscient observer;* or, as his afterthought
skeptically rehearsed on the way, perhaps to throw the first
stone at himself as chance propagator of his own fiction.
After ringing, Little heard a musical rush behind the door.
"Would *be* whippets," he guessed. Mrs Betur opened it.

Two young boxers sat at the threshold and with compassionate eyes on the strangers blocked their entrance. "Sib,
Gesib—they're brother and sister both innocent—please
step aside first and let these people in. My Georgia father
owned a racing stable. May be for that reason they run like
colts thru this apartment. They're gentle." Her manner was
arch, ladylike and hospitable. The boxers instantaneously
rose to the height of Little, the bodice of his mother, and to
one third the lean height of Baballo—and stepped aside,
that is in front of a waiting room on a line with the entrance. Mrs Betur evidently spoke English, but its registers,
suggesting somehow the foreign inflections of world-
travelled musicians in a large city, made it uncertain
whether her background referred to the Georgia of our
South or Gruziya. Verchadet waited a good part of a year
before Mrs Betur herself verified that it was precisely At-
lanta, "way back," before Sherman.

"Mr Betur will come out presently. His lunch is cooling, but he's had no time," she said drawing back the scarlet tasseled and festooned portieres that served instead of a door to the waiting room. Turning to it, so that the boxers now waited behind in the narrow hall down which they had raced, the von Chulnts could not help noticing a large dining room with beige festoon-blinds half-raised to let the sun in. It shone on a long Florentine lacecovered table set with goodies between appointed crystal stemware and two tall matching carafes sparkling with wine—red and white. "You're welcome to help yourselves whenever you come," Mrs Betur waved unpretentiously toward the display whose sunlit existence had potentially fed the von Chulnts' reserved appetites. Out of habit they declined with triple thanks and grace—and noticed further that the near end of the dining room, like the entrance on a line with the waiting room, was closed by heavy sliding doors. They sensed Betur's studio behind these, tho only a hurried rustling of sheet music reached them from the other side.

They entered a den where a softly lampshaded night eclipsed day. Crowded by two grand pianos, arranged curve to curve, and a row of club chairs, all three walls mounted a continuous collection of portraits of violin virtuosi and their signatures under glass framed by one-half-inch black borders of wood. To Little, the earliest going back a few centuries, when the idea of violin virtuoso first came to life, appeared to have just signed their autographs thru table-rapping hands. "How wonderful!" he said. "It's a bit chilly," Dala whispered. They walked around in the little space there was, studying them, as Verchadet tried to sit back in one of the club chairs much too big for her, thinking at the same time that it would be hard to get up again. From under the festooned portieres the boxers made their way to her and leaned their heavy heads affectionately against her legs and in the ample space to either side of them in the club chair. She had always felt kindly towards dogs but was shy of them. But they were all distracted then by a few measures of a Bach sonata played in the studio. "Out of tune," it was Little's turn to whisper. They heard the sliding doors open and a student's confident voice, "What Bach shall I bring the next time, Professor Betur?" —and the master's quieting voice: "What Bach? Any Bach."

If his reply sounded indifference, sound disappeared when he appeared. Bōwing, the slightest stoop, he seemed not to bōw. He held back the scarlet portieres for them by way of greeting, silent: taller than Baballo, younger than they expected, raven curled hair which the Western reader thinking of Romeo might attribute to Laila's Majnun. His dark eyes perhaps hinted at a smile forbidden to his lips.

An intimate downward glance at the boxers—no audible signal—was needed to make them get up and walk back with great dignity down the hall they had come from to unseen spaces in the apartment. Led politely by Betur thru the sunlit dining room the von Chulnts crossed the track of the opened sliding doors into a much larger room lit by standing lamps in broad day, then the sliding doors were shut. The studio's dazzling artificial night ended in rounded bays and a by now familiar shade of scarlet curtains—drawn. They bulged with a wind from the open windows behind them. Verchadet and Baballo were chilled at once.

They were reminded of daylight only by some motes trapped in a sunbeam across the white plastered ceiling bordered with carved rosettes. Looking down from these as it were—with an impression of being raised on his toes beyond the immediate clutter of furniture—Betur said: "Too much smoke, now too much *drepts*." The elder von Chulnts remained standing tacitly grateful when he walked over to shut one or two of the unseen windows responsible (as they understood him) for the *drafts*. He returned to his previous stance near drawers of music files, stacks of loose music, an executive's flat-topped desk heaped with papers, elegant writing gear and not so elegant stubs of pencils and variegated crayons, several cartons of cigarettes of different brands, and so on, all hiding the gloss of mahogany underneath but removed in some kind of personal order from a large sheet of graph paper apparently his schedule. The other furnishings of the room were too evident but obviously necessary: a concert grand with its partly unrolled rubber and brown canvas cover, weighted with more stacks of music, several violins and or in their cases; a tall bookcase with heavy tomes, placed directly in front of the fireplace and hiding its antique marble mantelpiece; a vast plum velvet sofa with several commensurate armchairs of a matching softness. "Please," he said indicating these.

The von Chulnts sat down. Betur stood. "Mr Endor called me, and has explained. I un'stand you wish my advice. In the situation it would be difficult," he said.

Verchadet assumed that "the situation" meant Athens, and quickly summed up Little's case as against Athens' own statement of his impasse as teacher. She emphasized that for Little it meant there would be no returning.

"I know Mr Olympus," Betur said, "we were fellows at the Conservatory. I'm sure it was on'y a misun'standing easily mended." He looked towards Little, who showing his best behavior looked back and said nothing.

The foreign professor's mixture of excellent English, solecisms and speech impediment puzzled Verchadet as much as his reluctance. Obviously what he did not wish to hear he did not hear. Nevertheless she was certain he had heard her and even respected her as contender—"after his kind" as the Scriptures say. What with a prospect of scales depressing her by this time she was ready to advance her Little. Dala gratuitously interjected for her: "Mr Warlock, as you know, believes that your method is indispensable to our son's debut, but as impresario he assures us of our son's talent. Tho we're his parents, we don't expect your assurance that you will make an artist of him, if by the age of twelve he doesn't show that he is enough of one to go on alone—without a teacher. Until then if you will teach him technique that is all we ask." Dala's wisdom or idiocy as a really omniscient observer might see it—especially his use of Endor's first name and the words "by the age of twelve" —left no more change on Betur's face than the sunbeam on a rosette overhead, which everyone in the room for an instant seemed to eye. Betur gazed above Baballo and turned to Verchadet: "You see, I don't prepare anyone for a debut. I just teach, and in recent years my *shedule* has been too full to accept boy*s*" (the last word ending in a soft *s*). "Still if you wish I'll hear him." Unexpectedly he addressed Little: "Play me."

"Bach?" Little asked firmly.

"For me that's not important. De Bériot?"

Betur had called for an old war horse concerto that young violinists must learn if they expect to become virtuosi. Little had mastered it and, tho *he'd* have preferred to play Bach, proceeded leisurely after an indifferent look to open his fiddle case, unswathe his half-size from its satin sack, remove his bow from its clamps, eye its straightness and tighten it, by which time Baballo tense over having to hear *that piece* he could not bear to hear again could have sworn that Betur's lowered gaze at the procedure betrayed impatience. It might be saying: young man, to save time my students do all that best on the street, or before entering my studio. How could the strange Betur divine that Snorckie's unhurried preparation was his way of letting the De Bériot flow thru him?

"Does the *modder* wish to accompany," the teacher asked. "No," she answered. Not wasting words Betur transformed into apocalyptic accompanist gave Little his *A*, made sure of the boy's tuning and they were off—if not abreast, not in tandem.

Betur stormed the piano with the orchestral part and

flooded it with wrong notes, on purpose as Little suspected, to throw him off pitch. Obviously Betur could wake up in the middle of the night to play any part of this score to fulfill any peer's test of his mastery of it. In the violin part Little kindled his own fireworks, wherever Betur leaped or skipped furiously turning, almost tearing pages—not playing them straight thru much as Little hoped he would, all the glides, slides, heralded coloratura of a century gone before Little was born: obdurately always in pitch. For once Dala, insensitive to Betur's wrong notes, appreciated the musical structure of the piece despite himself. During a cadenza Betur rose from the keyboard and danced as he stood in place, eyes, arms, hands, quickened breath, once catching himself singing, icon of Byzantine saint and Kurdish awe—the historic observer in Dala hopelessly looking for metaphor—what—before vandals covered the mosaics of Santa Sophia, brilliants long before the vulgar glutton's *come hither, shishke bab.* Never, never vulgar.

"Ver' talented poy," Betur said to the parents, "but it would be difficult with my present *shedule.* If you are sure as to Mr Olympus—there is no *horry,* he is *gut*—maybe I can arrange with Dr Presha my assistant, *moch* better, *moch* more patient than I with *yong* people, and I could hear your son *wance* a *manth."* Verchadet, who knew honest art— whatever the artist might be when she saw his "merchandise," a word for which she would thank Betur in the future —"would rather *arrange* now, to save time," she said. So it was agreed.

Dala, who paid his bills immediately and would rather diffuse into a dew than suffer the touch of money between himself and those he respected, had moved shyly with wallet in hand to Betur. "Please, no—not for advice—there is no reason this time," Betur said. Dala's eyes still offered— yet as it is sometimes generous to accept he accepted. But he was quite aware of the extravagance of his tastes—such as giving of himself to his bluebook students, or paying ten dollars (having misread the price tag as one dollar) for a six-inch square of Irish linen handkerchief for Verchadet who knew more about finance than he, or buying Snorckie a unicorn for his birthday—and honor gave him courage to venture *sotto voce:* "May I ask what is your fee?" "It would be half the usual, but I shall *probeably* be able to arrange a scholarship at *wan* or th'other of the institutions I teach in," Betur said simply.

Thru all this session Betur had spoken only the words *play me* to Little. Obviously part of his method was to demonstrate, not to talk. But he now turned to Little and asked, "What is your name?" "Little Baron." Betur smiled down and they shook hands. "He is to play only scales until I see him. To hold one note for a long time is the hardest," he said to Verchadet, who took this information to heart while looking at Little. He nodded. After the door closed on thank you's, he still seemed content.

In the subway its din in her ears prophesied a shadowy evening of rattling off musical scales. Dala, on his own time before another evening class completed his long day, transliterated, on his wallet's memo pad, from *Gorhoffedd* of Hywel ab Owain Gwynedd:

is the dent roc towered

15

Teeth help to keep the tongue quiet was Welshman Gwynedd's literal meaning.

Dr Vasily Presha's troubled small white teeth, misleading a foreign man with an ailing heart, did not stop him from speaking too much. Researchist in the French style of violin bōwing, whose method he had fed to Betur's more instinctive use of it, Presha often remarked how much better Imam had fared since their young days as equals. *"Nu, zat's natural,"* he memorialized in concluding a story or lesson. *"My fāter wass Proshian,"* he told Verchadet, "but I'm *Roshian*. Betur and myself *ferst studded in Roshia*. Nu, zat's natural."

How *natural* anyone with a sense for status, after having been at Imam's, could see on coming to Vasily's. Little entered Presha's studio crossing his one threshold into the squeezed long end of *one* room, as he judged at once from a lid of ceiling which extended beyond yet weighed over this area. In itself it formed a narrow proscenium between a row of leaded windows and a purple divider of thick folds of curtain hung from heavy brass rods along its entire length. Three highbacked overstuffed armless armorial chairs were backed against the windows. An iron violin stand, a marble and ormolu table completed the properties. Not until summer, in another setting after a winter of discontent, would Little solve the mystery behind the curtain. It was Mrs Presha's domain and (*as if Shakespeare had anything to do with it,* as Little would then tell Lada) her *printless* flight while her husband taught. "Dear *Blume,* Mr Presha pronounces it as in Heine, is a beautiful woman," Mrs Betur would soon tell Verchadet. "She still studies singing, her lifelong ambition's to act Carmen, and she very well does her by twining a rose in her hair or flinging it." On his part, Vasily's preamble to Little's very first lesson with him also hinted at flaws that prolong friendships: "Ada Betur give up violin when she married Imam." Not that Verchadet was curious to hear about it—she dreaded gossip.

The lesson proceeded. "Imam wass ver' imprest, ver' angshoes to have—" (Little's name?) "f'r pupil. Wass afred you no come, he loose, like on stock market, he said, can happens. He toll me," he turned to Verchadet, "won'r'ful ta-lent, stronk character. I say him, Imam, all-wace you say *wait, they come.* You cam. Nu, zat's natural.

"Ass far me," he turned back to Little, "I titch then he take you. Far me iss all-wace from the beg-inning. Bot dis ferst time, play me!" After Presha's disclosure of Betur's anxiety, *play me* echoed Imam to Little.

"*The Devil's Trill?*" he asked.

"What-you-want," Dr Presha said, picking up his own heavy fiddle as for an emergency. He had opened his collar on giving Little free choice. A small golden cross hung from his broad white neck as he tuned softly now and then while Little played, deadpan but checking on him as well. "Humidt af-fects," Presha sweated, obviously annoyed and breathing with effort. "Out! out!" he'd say vehemently from time to time, elbowing, forearm forward.

As I'm doing all along, Little thought, where does he think my arm is—prepared to hear him say, "Nu, zat's nat-ural," as he finished the piece to his own satisfaction. He was not prepared for insult.

"Not moch ima-jinn-ation," Presha said. "I don't hear what Imam—. Needs mat-urity. Bot f'me pieces not interesting."

"You're no jinn *eyether*," Little looked away silently, wondering about Presha's short pronunciation of *ie* in *pieces* and Dala's confidential advice on such matters.

"Far me it's the bōwing wrong. Not so moch trouble with finger-rink. See, ev-ery stroke, ferst leetle, den more, mo-re, more-moch presha." He stressed the increase of pressure with bōwed-out knees and fiddle sagging to the floor. "Iss hard. Nu, zat's natural. We have sayink in Roshia: feedink de peegs t'honor de livink."

Had Baballo been there the saying would have reminded him of his sister, Murda-Wonda—her pitiless capacity for suffering, only *she* was not male.

"What do you think," Little asked Verchadet, once out of earshot of Presha.

"What do you?" she asked *him*.

"If it leads to Betur maybe?"

After an Institute *function* Dala was walking home with an equally questionable variant of Gwynedd:

is that eye hant rack toward—

16

"Rather life is longwinded, art is winded," Dala reverted, compassionate over Little but hoping for his sympathy. Now six, Little, sitting, looked up—with as much established maturity as most humans ever need have—and said: "Ah peeg-poet h-it saze in my hoss-Roshian science't's book-a in quesh-wan-able Een-glish, *We live in an ocean of air with our feet on the ground.* It's almost boring," he confided, "no, not the scales, the feesh"—he rose to enact the authority sagging to the floor—"*Preh-eh-eh-sha!*—Dala."

But the month came round. After three lessons with Presha, the family were all together again at Betur's. Little played the G-flat major scale—and perhaps the C-sharp minor—Verchadet wasn't listening when Betur leaped suddenly and said: "I take him." Except for promising "a piece in *a-nodder manth*" he said nothing else. So till then it was back to Presha.

Finding another occasion, "we don't seem to sit together or talk much these days," Dala said sitting down next to Little. "Read me a *Sonnet*, Dala," Little said, his head heavy on Dala's shoulder. "Don't bother to *fetch*—I feel so Een-glish—your *Complete Plays and Poems*. My little vest-pocket leather one of the *Sonnets* is right here next to *Babar* and *Leopold Mozart*." "Which?" Baballo asked, stretching his free hand to pick up last year's Christmas volumette of

Shakespeare's *unannotated Sonnets,* inscribed *from Little to Lada.* "77," Little said.

"Good," he said when Dala had finished, his head nestled heavier on Dala's clavicle. "Won't your head ache that way, son?" Dala asked with no intent to stir him. "No, it's just right. What were *you* reading, Dala, before *77?*" "O— *My Institute News.*" "The new issue—is it funny? Read a bit of it, Dala?"

His father leaned back ever so slightly in the little spindle-back rocker, so as not to show himself bucking the transfixions in his collarbone, and after half a breath read:

> A trough of the enrollment wave was reached in 1949, and it is this class which has just graduated. This fall there are already twenty-five paid deposits. Dr Kite whose studies of natural products especially nucleic acids, with the ultracentrifuge, are internationally known. The present Institute represents a continuation and expansion of the Shellac Bureau, supported by Importers Associates, which has carried out practical tests of the solubility of various types of shellacs, its adhesion to certain base metals, and other properties. Investigations by Winger, Hotch, and Yodbull and new applications of natural rubber ingraft copolymers. Dr. Conrad Cubinis, who now spends three-fourths of his day in his bathtub, appeared briefly at yesterday's meeting, admitting he was somewhat fagged from deep salt studies.

"And is that why he had a dream, as he told you, of a hurricane warning in Chinatown, his *lowers* blown off, turning to face a faceless Chinee, shrieked and fell off the bed?" asked Snorckie. "Maybe," said Baballo.

"Are there any student letters?" Little asked.

"One—and it's signed *I. Count Jr.*—which reminds me of your young cousin—years since I've seen him, I should. It reads:

I am happy to be in the Institute, but still not resigned to your Humanities program. Why should
I be, considering my world. Prior to being a Vet I
didn't go to college partly because I was sure I'd
be drafted. Maybe I thought it'll build me up
physically—if it does, there'll be some good in it.
I've learned since like almost everybody else who
read a book overseas that your Humanities list is
the same as the Army's, part of the setup of a world
that will ultimately come out of a test tube and be
so refined and 'beautiful' it'll just die."

"Will they be tested first?" Little asked—and then,
"it's always touching when a good man uses the word *beautiful*. How moving he can be." Not sure that Little meant
what he said seriously, Dala nodded affirmatively.

"And how are President Gluck Coma, Dean Kittenhoare, and Chairman Rumples?" Little asked.

"About the same," Dala said, "they have all, from
Coma down, asked me to take on another assignment."

"Have there been any rumors—" "of a raise? no. It
wouldn't do to assault them. It's harder to be unkind. Why
should one be ungenerous, tho I suppose they also think of
themselves and find quiet easier, as I do," Dala said, noticing that Little glanced with impatience.

Outside the house a neighborly radio abruptly blared a
commercial, *o what a beautiful morning, o what a beautiful
day.* "Must be Henry Filler taking out the garbage, he car-
ries his portable everywhere these days," Little said of his
yearsmate, who—the blare stopped—was done with the
chores of this evening.

"I was thinking, Dala, of our situations and 77 and
time's thievish progress," Little said, "only scales and no
music for days yet, and with so much time on my hands I've
(quote) *enriched* my diary with some writing." Something
had changed and Dala felt sad: Little *had* said *diary.*

"(quote) *To take a new acquaintance of thy mind.* If

(quote) *thou wilt look,* Dala—under *Leopold* there—and hand me my old *dairy*—thank you. It's a what do you call it, mostly a mummy play—a mummer's play?—a mummy play. And if you will read it so to speak (quote) *from thy brain,* I can judge better of its (quote) *blacks,* not *blanks* as my poor text misprints. Never mind my spelling and handwriting, just edit these—unvoiced—as you read aloud." Dala read as instructed.

FRIENDS—GLOCKENSPIEL, RUMPLES & FATHER XMAS

(Pump and circummarch, enter omnes)

FATHER XMAS. Glockenspiel, Rumples—and Father Christmas.
(Exit Xmas. Glocke and Rumples salute with candystripe canes.)

RUMPLES. Pshu—we build house.

GLOCKE. Pshu—*(admires while* RUMPLES *exits and enters with galleon can of paint and giant jar of putty.)* What color? *(opens gallon)* Good. Now we hose! Go buy me steel wool—but what color, Rumples? Red—yellow hay blue—

RUMPLES. Shu' *(walks off)*

GLOCKE *(yelling after him)*. No, bring me black!
*(*RUMPLES *returns with black)* I'm sorry I meant to say brown. Go bring that back!

(Scaena. A store, Glocke on doorstep)

RUMPLES. Oh he really meant brown!

GLOCKE. What'n hell, Rumples!

RUMPLES. Gr r

GLOCKE. I can't help you. Go to *this* store, it sears. Not this store, *this* store.

RUMPLES. What color? Oi wus idus!

(exeunt omnes)

Epilogus
FATHER XMAS (with KITTENHOARE)

my days at the zoo
are to few
I wonder what
this means to you

the seals   shivers
make my quivers
all an'mules from lion to monkey
are in the zoo
except the donkey

we're of the zoo
to hear the lion roar
sincerely your
new universal vacuum corps

> (*pump and circummarch,*
> *exeunt omnes*)

"*Explicit?*" Dala asked—in his mind helping a late Latinist with his coat—"tho there seems to be more here under *Mozart*—an epilogue to an epilogue?" he hesitated.

"Oh no!" Little looked down at an old page he had forgotten was out of place. "Juniorviler," he said for *juvenilia*, "don't you remember, I wrote that almost two years ago." They read together silently:

Who doesn't like Mozart's *Lullaby* and Papageno and *A Minuet*, and *Ah vous dirai-je maman* and *The Sonatina*, or does not remember Leopold carrying the baby Wolfgang downstairs and the Prince asking about him? When Mozart was five Leopold taught him the violin. He wrote arithmetick, or numbers, all over the wall because there was no paper in that day. One evening when his father and two old cronies—their names alas long forgotten—were playing trios Wolfgang asked to join them for quartets. "You may play but very softly," his father said, "so nobody hears you." But Leopold's love was not abated. He couldn't

believe his eyes, because little Mozart played every
single note.

"That was about the time you spoke to the collie, who
barked only at night, and complained, almost whined, *he
doesn't answer me.*"

"Pshu," Little said, and closed the diary, "you put too
much expression into it. Dala," he raised his voice as one
might say compulsively, "you're more of a child than I am
—do an imitation after all these years?" "Which one," his
father answered aware now that his collarbone had fallen
asleep, and gladly rising from the rocker, "J.D.Sr. with his
dime and golden throat, or Wozzeck *zeig mir deine Zunge,*
or Papa Leopold?"

"Ach lieber Papà, gewiss heute es Leopold sein müsst,"
Little pleaded to encourage Dala's equally fantastic German.

At once, half his height, bent under an imaginary peri-
wig, Papa Mozart beseeched him: "Fliessender Sohn,
Wol-l-f-gang! wo hast du meine sperlingseule geige verfluch-
tet, mit den bogen, mit den gehobenen bogen, nicht dein
spielzug achtel, meine geige mit'n stolzen bogen, ach zau-
berhaft, ach magisch, hochherzigkeit, entweder entweich-
end entwendend 'ch habe gesucht in die gewölbte Decke, in
die Wände und sinke den Flur an—und so forsch wahn-
sinnig—"

One morning as Baballo sat writing, still unrushed before his one noon hour of teaching of that day, Little thru with his own stint of scales and ancient history was moved to teach *him*. Looking down over his father's shoulder, he read and said: "I agree, 'Aside from amazing things writers do with genius, I don't believe they have said the first sensible thing about the melodic and other meanings of words in their relations.' But all this about—'in music seven notes may be sharped and flatted, or it's another scale of five or twelve or higher multiple of tones in relation, but words are not multiples of tones (or are they?) and presumably endlessly related'—is nonsense: partick'r'ly from somebody who admits he can't count higher than three, and never in equal time." "I agree," Baballo said, "that's what I'm getting to."

Little offered *himself*, "May I ever teach you the fiddle, Dala, tho you always pick up the bow with your left hand? You could start with the piano, an instrument which I don't especially respect, its keys are always there to lap one up. Come Dala, sit down at the piano." That much Dala did, snorted, baffled like someone who is tickled, then balked: "It's no use, Snorckie, I wouldn't even attempt it, I have two left hands," and looked up with reverence. "Ah, you need *teem-merity* of musical attack," Little considered, "ancient history tells me you're no Memnon. When the sun struck, *he* harped back: action and reaction. Physics: if a stone plays possum to trip me I go back and kick it"—as Dala agreed he had seen Little do. "A string breaks, I restring. A fiddle needs playing *in* before it plays. It fights its bouts before it sings." Again Dala agreed and added, "the word is *temerity*, Little."

Verchadet, who had just stepped in from looking at the crab apple blossoms, overheard Dala's scrupulous diction, and not anxious to engage discussion said, "you're two of a kind," and walked out.

"Not to put you to shame in front of Verch," Little went on, "I adventure to say there's as much variety of timbre— pronounced *tam'b'r* in music—as there are trees before they become confused in one stupid word like *timber*. Lada Dala should know, *The man that hath no music in himself, Let no such man be trusted. Better can* teach wood. *Zo:* I've written a short treatise for students such as Presha. Obviously it is not meant for me. What I like about writing is the mystery of how it turns out. It (quote 77) *shall profit thee,* before I come back for your first lesson."

Little left to join Verchadet in the garden, and Dala stayed on alone to read:

THE YOUNG VIOLINIST
for Curt Budder

(INSERT) figure 1. violin with arrows to parts
figure 2. bow showing tip, hair, frog

Scales

Number	Sharps ♯	Flats ♭
1	G	F
2	D	B♭
3	A	E♭
4	E	A♭
5	B	D♭
6	F♯	G♭
7	C♯	C♭

Scales are important to those who know music. Look up at the table to scale number 1. Which is it, first or second? (answer.)

The eighth note of the scale is always the octave. (Number 1) G is the eighth from G. The reason why the eighth is always like the one is: the eighth to the one is an octave and one to eight is an octave. So you can see what is meant by an octave.

Now try it on the C major scale, or if you don't have it ask your mother, if she's a musician, to buy it. (Scale books are very expensive, you never know how much they charge.) When you have the C major scale, ask yourself which is the eighth C and the first C.

satis quod sufficit

Practice

The young violinist keeps his violin in a case. His mother prepares the room for practice. When he is ready he tunes, or she must try to turn the pegs. (figure 1)

An hour or two at one time of very hard practice is *in effect all the time*—as the great Ztephiah, whose teacher was Dlopoel Reua, cautions. In any case, don't just run thru everything because you are consciously mad, but proceed slowly. (No rewards—except: if the practice is good and the weather sunny the violinist's mother *may* urge him to fix the swing in the yard as inducement to more practice.)

Any bow (figure 2) can be heavy enough, especially a heavy bow. The popular entertainer's way of holding the bow at the tip and weighing it down with the frog does not show a sensitive player, nor does nervous stroking of the hair as a proof of its being rosined. Both of these actions are probably caused by early training that encourages constant yelling and screaming. (As a child this writer attended a school where a missing piece of picture puzzle led to such fighting and screaming to find it his health was nearly impaired. He went home, with no love for picture puzzles, to listen to his fiddle, and never returned to that school.)

Music to Play

Scales, exercises, concertos, sonatas, etc—is the ancient orderly course of study. But depending on competence or musicality—and most often in practice this holds oppositely for student and teacher —if competent, scales and exercises; if musical, mostly *etc*, which includes concertos and sonatas. Especially musical teachers and students will of course confer with other treatises or between themselves.

Little never again mentioned his treatise, which Baballo stored with his own papers. Either too modest to presume on musicality or whatever it was in himself that involved him in it generally, habit had convinced him he was not the kind who sits down to confer with a piano.

Betur who might have suspected Little was capable of a treatise never read it, but must have felt it coming. It was late spring when he made good his promise to have Little enrolled, at some saving to Baballo, in *wan* of the institutions where, in the opinion of less silent musical colleagues, Betur's prestige as distinguished teacher transfigured his competence. "Apart from my lessons and Dr Presha's," Betur explained with enigmatic judgment to Little, "the *on'y odder* obligation of the course of study is that the administration needs theory, but *wan* hour on *Sat'day* won't take away too *moch* time."

Verchadet and Dala were present at Little's matriculation—waiting behind a closed door during his placement test for the theory course. To Baballo, as much as he could overhear, it consisted largely of marching in step and metronomic rappings. When the elderly, severe yet sympathetic lady who taught theory stepped out for a moment during the short written examination and stopped to ask them what they wanted, Baballo could not help saying gallantly, "I am afraid one of your minors who is having his difficulties." She responded with a silent hauteur of a veteran teacher, so that let down he felt, as in a recurrent dream of his childhood, he had spoken in class out of turn. The examination qualified Little for Theory IV. As there was no such class in the undergraduate school, he would be registered in Theory III, "for the duration beginning in the fall," he told Verchadet.

But the musical year had not ended she learned at Betur's last lesson before the awaited summer. "A violinist accomplishes most in summer, along with vacation," Betur advised her as they were saying good-bye. Lessons would be free if Little could attend his summer school at Garden. *"Op* state," he added—"Little is too *yong* to board at school where parents are not allowed, but *ludging* involves compensation, perhaps the family could instead rent a place for vacation in Pamphilia not far away. It would be good for everybody."

18

Dala was thinking about Sumer when Little told him and Verchadet he supposed they *should go.* They went.

"Welcome to the human race—the bon mot is Mr Betur's greeting. You *are* Mr and Mrs von Chulnt and Little?" The blond lady, in her thirties and her paler blond replica about eleven, tall for her age but pretty out of a fairy book Little and Verchadet thought, were reassured by his violin case before the attired and travelled had quite stepped down from the train. After ten hours of spur track along the river and lakes north of it Baballo breathed mountain air, looking straight up at a span of blue—prolonging day. But he interrupted himself soon enough to say to the lady: "Yes, how very kind of you, we were thinking of taking a taxi."

"I am Lambeth Potiphar—my daughter, Unzung Pharette. And it's our third summer at Garden. Unzung's father Dr Potiphar teaches surgery in Constantinople—Istanbul—but we're native. I was thinking—our youngsters are so fortunate having Mr Betur for their teacher. He happened to mention you were not coming up in a car, and as Pharette has a neuritic finger from practicing vibrato we've taken his advice to do some shopping here in Piraeus and meet your train. May we give you a lift into Pamphilia? The town does not have any taxi service, tho a seasonal arrangement can be made with private owners of sedans. But the five mile drive there with you should be so much more delightful for us." "Do we go past Garden?" Little asked. "No, Garden is five miles further north from the house you will stay in in Pamphilia—ours is across the bridge from yours," Unzung Pharette replied. "Rentals are scarce in Pamphilia. Mr Betur has sixty students and most families rent a year ahead," Mrs Potiphar said. "A few years from now, when our youngsters are of an age to stay at the dormitory in Garden, perhaps we old folk can stay home. We were almost too late to keep our place this year. I had intended to spend the summer in Turkey, but Unzung could not bear to think of leaving Mr Betur for so long a spell." The von Chulnts crouched too obviously for courtesy in getting into the accommodating car. Little took over the conversation which diverted to preventives and cures for Unzung's injury. She stared kindly and listened to him as to a much older authority. So understanding for her age, girls mature faster, Verchadet considered, warding off a yawn. She was shocked when Mrs Betur told her a week later that Unzung Pharette had tacitly celebrated "sixteen plus" some time ago.

"A castle!" Little looked with wonder across the highway from their new address where Mrs Potiphar's sedan had stopped to let them out. His elders looked also: behind a long town block of rock wall, hedge, a private bridge arched over a natural moat created by a fast running stream, ended in high ground, lawn, meadow; led to ascending woods, a mountain—in the foreground a castle. "The family estate of Lieutenant Governor Castle—he died last year. Yes, you have a pretty view—." Mrs Potiphar admired it. "We must go home presently, to a half-hour of healthy détaché—as Mr Betur urged—without vibrato, Pharette? We'll let you good people settle in, and meet you refreshed no doubt at the post office tomorrow, just below the Castle estate down the highway in our direction. There's only one incoming mail, at noon—'bye." "Bye." Mrs Potiphar effected part of her U-turn for home in the driveway along the side porch of the house still unopened by Baballo's new key. Little effected—*"that, there—open!"*

Meanwhile Verchadet looked around at the single choice writing several letters had offered her. Evening recalled shades of Riding Hood. She lit the bare electric bulb of the front porch. The house of three stories, too high for its width fairly rambled upward with porches and verandas —those at the rear and shaded side evidently storage space for the landlord's old bedsprings and broken furniture. They decided at once to use only the ground floor, unless Dala himself wished to clean up one of the upper verandas as a retreat for thought. (He did in time.) As always, Little's room was readied first, so they could fuss with their rooms alone while he slept "sensibly," he said, "like anybody sane." They went on cleaning and ordering long after midnight, startled by glares from cars making their U-turns over cinders of their driveway—confusing the flashes at first with summer lightning. Finally before drinking a sixth coffee, which they intended to enjoy sitting down, they dismounted seventeen highly colored reproductions of martyrdom in heavy gold frames and stored them in the pantry— beyond use to them—Dala carefully noting from which walls they came so he could hang them again when their vacation was up.

"Pamphilia among rocks and falls," Little greeted them out of his guide book, with the light, birds and his open violin case. With Betur in mind he said, "I see you have *accomplishèd* old curtains after working all night." Verchadet sipped her coffee, wondering, as the sun shone in, if the flimsy lawn curtains exposed the distasteful living room to the highway. Her worry could not have been justified sooner. They heard a gentle rapping, and the shadow of a head pressed against the outside of front porch window. All three went to the door together.

"Good morning. Today will be lovely. I hope I am not very early. I shall be your fortunate neighbor in the house next to yours—I hardly leave my porch. Mrs Potiphar told me I will hear a violin again. I thought about it all night—the happiness for me—and fortified myself to thank your dear little son. You must be very good to study with Mr Betur. It was wonderful in the years before Mr Betur moved his school to Garden—violins sounding all over Pamphilia. I'm afraid most people here didn't think so. They'd rather drive their cars to hear the music in Garden on Saturday night. But I'm too old for the concerts, more content to listen here—as I was a half-hour ago. I must not disturb you and go now. Do when you have time say hello —I'm nearly always on the porch." The small country lady with hunched back and thick coils of white braided hair turned slowly to follow her cane home. She had not given her name. "She seems *content*—quote, unquote—to forget it," said Little, "let's just call her Mrs Weatherbureau."

She proved loyal to the surname: beginning indeed later that morning, recalling by their titles the pieces Little had practiced and forecasting exactly what weather the afternoon would bring: it happened for their part they had encouragingly nodded to her porch a half-flight of stairs above ground. Thanks to her the von Chulnts were made conscious of weather all summer. Except for rainy days when she listened indoors they missed no forecast. Snorckie warned against inviting themselves to her house. He could not forget her first and only actual intrusion on their privacy. An old lady's happiness and weather reports were not his reasons for practice. "She should try playing a fiddle herself and see if it's bliss—or do some other work," he insisted.

What baffled Little was that *work* in Pamphilia meant everyone minded somebody else's work. Greeting the von Chulnts anywhere, without having met them before, seemed to be a great part of this work. "Their main *bitzness*, including the druggist's," Little whispered to be overheard, "is that I am a violinist." He asked Verchadet if she thought Betur was to blame for this "adwanz spying." She reserved her opinion, while in her mind Betur's bon mot about the human race implied a contest or just running, that at some time she must be as wary as he was. Dala was always so impersonally puzzled Little did not bother to ask *his* opinion. "The best he could do," Little said, "is to appear naked at the porch window or the door and drive them off when they peer or knock. But No-oh! He can never refuse a fool the *hoarsepitality*" (a good pun as he heard it) "of his living room especially when his *leetle* boy is playing Mozart and for some nosey reason a fool wants to hear it!"

To blame or not for Snorckie's annoyance, in Pamphilia Imam Betur whether worshipped or feared "was legend." Sponsorial (or vicarious) rather than not the human race gathered at the post office, and when the von Chulnts arrived hopefully to pick up their one letter from Tearilee or Murda-Wonda they were cornered by throwbacks to Babel. "With only one intention," Snorckie insisted, "to find out our Betur connections, as if we don't know they gossip." Their talk always involved in Imam "pounced" at Little, as he had to face it, from three types of "ambush": that of the infants Betur still weaned or almost had weaned into perpetual youth, some weary in their thirties with their parents and pianists while Betur worked mostly with his mouth shut; Betur's public at the Saturday night concerts, folk who had not "studied" the violin, but "loved" and were dedicated to support it with charity and sentiment—like the help at Garden whose ancestors had left them heirloom fiddles or equivalent fortunes, and in contrast to these somewhat extinguished, musical doctors, dentists, artists and writers reputedly "great"—summering at a near Indian reservation—but only one songstress, Mrs Presha; last and *foremost*, as Little had heard, two rival impresarios (one of them Endor) who vaguely "visited," and more openly their "patrician" virtuosi who *had made it*. The rumors were they had been brought up or sent by the impresarios so Betur could finger for them some lately commissioned concerto. Their flying from Battersea to Helsinki had left them no time or taste to finger it on their own.

Ceaseless tales of Imam: Little recorded the personal annoyances in his *dairy*.

Three Ambushes or The Envious Variations
(spelling by an omniscient observer)

Ambush I
Lambeth with her blossom Unzung: "Goo'd morning, and how are you this mourning? *We're* so overjoyed. Pharette has just come back from her first lesson. The school's not officially open. This was a make-up lesson we had come up for, a week early, postponed you know by the accident to her forefinger." (I'm sure she said yesterday they were almost too late to rent their place this year.) "Well—to heal the wounds Mr Betur has told her to *practice me good* Wieniawski's *Ecole Moderne*. That's advanced for exercises, isn't it, Little?" (To wound my heels—lurking to find out how advanced I'm.) "Oh! do meet the Rilty's and son Panza—violinist and best tackle on high school team." (Catty: to line me up against him. He's not Betur's pupil, Presha's best.)

Mrs Rilty: "Next year Panza will study mental music too." Broad education! "Maybe you can tell me," opening vile *Mixed Melodies* to a bit of Bach partita, "is this fingering for a boy or girl?" (Harmless? Also asked if my fiddle's dark or bright. To price it and me: thinks the best "violinists" are Stradivari or Guarneri. Itching for Panza to study with Betur.)

Mr Schwerscheide, old-school violin teacher: "I'd never let my Lona" (daughter, very nearsighted, not young) "study with that—*that* stableman Betur." She studies with Serp, Betur's rival, whose one great prodigy *was* Nihunem. She's his last pupil, besides his son, this summer in studio near Indian reservation.

Mr Noë and son Solo at private adjoining P.O. boxes: "Have you arranged for your lesson with Betur, Solo?" "*No!* I'm not taking lessons this summer." "No?" "*I told you* I'm going to relax playing in my orgon box. How do you expect me to have a sweet tone when Svengali snaps his fingers like B-B guns over me, *forcing* me to keep time without rubato? Fact is the fiend's grown gentle since he filliped his index finger into the middle of Josh Slider's forehead for a wrong note and he fainted. No lessons'll teach him a lesson." "So *with whom* will you study?" (abruptly to me) "I bet *you* think Mr Betur's a great teacher." (I smile politely.)

Mr Ambrose Flutit, Garden's chaperon pianist: "Mr Betur is *exhausted,* what with the two boxers chasing the porcupines and their having to stop at every comfort station coming up. And the two grand pianos still to be tuned not off the trailer— o my! Our first lesson may be delayed, Little." (Not too convincing. There's enough litchr'chew'r *for the violin alone.*)

Mrs Bearmeout, daughters Marj and May, 14 and 17: "We've just received a wonderful letter from Eichel Practice about his triumph in Antigua." (Eichel, 17 like May, Mrs B. probably thinking of a match with Betur's greatest prodigy to-date. All the fools here blabbing he outdoes Ztephiah. Due back in Garden soon. I'll hear.) "I keep urging

the girls, they don't listen to me, 13 hours practice a day did it." (31 hours wouldn't bear her up
or out.)

Dr and Mrs Cyclops and son Tremor: they model
his "own musicality" after Eichel's practice. "We
all have our own style, don't we, Little?" (A grudg-
ing greeting?)

Ambush II
Druggist tries to sell us the family heirloom. "Been
in the attic 40 years and goes back at least 40 years
futher." The violin looks like a Blutwurst.

Hushlushes, two gray sisters, have worshipped
Eichel "since he first took up the prenatal position"
—my mother's spry *hapax legomenon*—but really
that's all they talk about.

Miss Nasaltwang stays at Anthos style of hotel, tho
much quieter, grave-like, where Chamber of Com-
merce allows no violin practice. She's driven
around in a black Cadillac by her chauffeur Di-
orcle. Very cordial. Has offered to take us to Garden Saturday Night Concerts "whenever" her
"favorite little violinist Eichel plays." Chief interest's ethnic dances, but hopes I'm as good as
Eichel so she'll have *two* young violinists in Garden. Back in the city she attends—for her much
older friend's sake, Miss Nishgut—the Sinfoni
concerts and goes to hear the old virtuosi in Great
Hall. Both convinced the old are fading before
Eichel.

Mme Kupeh, the wife of Pamphilia's one doctor.
He came here with a fatal illness years ago, but
since there are too many patients refuses to show
it. Has no time for Garden, so Mme Kupeh gives a
big concert party every summer in *her* garden
where Betur and Serp, *both* her friends, can appear together with their students. This year it's a

benefit for Schwerscheide's Lona. The invitation reads, *Invited to hear great artistry.* All Garden's *registered,* as Betur calls his pupils, *must* go, if only to say later, "her pitch is so erratic, she hears less than she sees." Mme Kupeh, "gracious and active grandmother," also studies pots and paintings at Pamphilia's art school, *The Northern Propylaeum.* A tremendous shed, full of earthenware pots, bottles, portraits, and pepper-and-salt paintings of clipper ships on the St. Lawrence. The director Feminore Coupran, honorary member at the Royale Academy, has just accomplished, Mme Kupeh tells us, a remarkable likeness of Betur done all in various blues, and would like to paint me. All I have to do is to pose! When Dala and Verchadet said nothing, as I did, Mme Kupeh looked surprised and said, "Why, Eichel leaped at the honor."

"Unbelievably," to quote Mrs Presha. At last we have met her. She *is* Carmen. *Very gay:* "After wondering all spring behind the curtain what you looked like and how your fiddle bore up so nicely under Presha—but everybody in Pamphilia meets at the post office. Here there is nothing to do but practice and babble. I prefer my solfège or nothing —and the movies in the evening. I must show you where it is the first time. It's good for breathing, away from it all—one must have a vacation."

Mrs Otototot, elephant lady with chest arthritis— from trying on children's dresses and underwear: companion of the two ancient Mrs Hemdlach sisters, who own the only other castle in Pamphilia's outskirts. Exulting in highest praises of Betur she tells us as executrix (I wonder) of her old friends' charities that she is responsible "among other things, for the scholarships to Garden" and my free lessons. Betur will notify me soon, she surprises me, about my musicale at Hemdlach Castle. First I hear of it. Is it possible he trusts her between one belch ("pardon me") and another? She wants to be kissed hello and good-bye. Faugh! So far I've escaped by picking up my fiddle case.

Thru all this madness, sardonic (?) snardic Ira Taignit ("a great writer" I've heard from Mrs Rilty and Panza) smiles wordless from the darkest corner of the post office at the people coming and leaving. Mrs Potiphar says he has smiled that way for three years at the Saturday Concerts in Garden, disdainfully, not speaking to anybody, and not so much as a handshake for Betur.

Ambush III
No one's seen him tho everybody whispers Warlock's secretly visiting Garden.

En passant Caasi Nrets, Ztephiah's "most mature" rival for bookings (which Ztephiah refuses—to play tennis instead—he's so fed up) has nodded to us. Hear Betur has teased Nrets: "In *shut* the public is promiscu*os*. Come a midget and hoo-hah! Genius's alone, suffers mismanagement. You know what au*tt*ority is. Ztephiah plays with au*tt*ority. And you I un'stand—from your publtzity—*witt auttority!*" Nrets whose broad public smile winces a bit when he overhears someone talking of Eichel is a short man. Dala, coming out of the post office and almost stepping on Nrets' heels, recalls some Institute joke about some notable, so short he sued the civic authorities for laying a buckled pavement too near his *annus mirabilis*. It's all right for Dala to pun badly, he's so tall.

tuner   wresting   resting   wrest pins   oreful
                                   oarful

Guy Esor Octa Leber, black curly hair and only famous bass viol player in the world has psych'n' liced and formed the chamber music groups at Garden for this year: they include all the non-virtuosi who need encouragement.

I've met so many people, heard so many names, I wonder if I've really heard them or am making them up, reading backward as in a mirror—mirror fugue.

Eichel not hear yet.

19

The von Chulnts would not ask anyone to spare them the encumbrances of a Cadillac and its cabby owner who drove them to the weekly half-hour lessons in Garden and back. Nor did the meddlers watching the time of Little's departure and return offer their cars, as Mrs Potiphar had offered hers (Dala would not forget) once in Piraeus. On these self-supported drives the father sat next to the cabby, Verchadet and Little less responsive to summer drafts and chatter in the back seat where Little possessed his violin case. Perhaps it was during the second trip going the cabby said, "Curious —Mrs Potiphar—the name *Potiphar*, my Bible concordance says it means *belonging to the sun or gift of the risen one*. Professor von Chulnt, I've been meaning to ask, would you know if the unleavened bread, after the slaves went out of Egypt, was kneaded." Attentive and thwarted Dala shook his head the least bit from side to side—ignorant—and looked silently to the road ahead.

It approached them bumpy thru mountain, rock slides at its sides, passed under a ski coast, a deer hurtling, a scurrying porcupine, and widened flatly thru woods. "These woods have been felled many times," the cabby said, "but enough's still virgin." "How do you know it is virgin?" Little leaned subdued over his case to ask his father. "I guess—like the close columns of trees where there's no underbrush, no grass, no flowers, no ground cover." "I see." A freestanding wrought iron gate appeared, and in curlicue of the grille work GARDEN. "I'll wait for you on this side of the gate, you can walk round it," the cabby said.

Betur was a gardener *by nature,* as the expression prevails. "I (must) *moss,*" he once said to a colleague whose solicitude for Betur's health on an enforced day off over a bourbon had provoked him to a subtle fingering for the colleague, *"torch'r* (torture) the children I nurse— *moch too stronk the drink—wat iss?"* "He putters like a gardener it seems for an unbearable time and then something happens," the colleague would say. " 'Sopsurd (it's absurd)" Betur was given to say, "sometimes happens." The von Chulnt triad first saw Betur in Garden standing on the largest rock of his considerable circle of rock garden— a content profile of care—just to the other side of the freestanding gate. He must have heard the motor of the Cadillac, yet as tho it were better to go as Betur by ear, his eyes perhaps hinting impatience with some small flower slow to come up on the rocks, he did not turn. When he did he saw them, smiled and moved forward but stopped, holding his long hands away from himself only to cross them over his forearms, cradling them soiled with earth as an excuse. The triad waved at a distance: they were not the ones to press toward him. He waved back and hurried off to the two story sprawling house in the classical style of over a century ago, which they knew must be the dormitory and summer studio.

"He was not wearing his black *smokeative* jacket with the sashes," Little said. "His velveteen smock, Little," Verchadet laughed almost inaudibly, not too pleased by Betur's greeting, "perhaps he likes to be rustic in the country." Even Dala had an afterthought: "Well, it is not exactly the *fêtes galantes,* or is it?"

They were early for this first lesson and looked around they felt perhaps longer than Betur's reserved welcome prompted. But what they had taken to be the front of the house was the back. The front was a new tessellated terrace whose granite balustrade crenelated a precipice above checkered green upland and red barns. They were surprised, looking down judging a drop of one thousand feet, that this was the entrance to Garden as well as one end of its wooded plateau.

As they turned to face the woods again Mrs Betur coming out of a long shed under these at the side of the main house hurried to greet them. Ada—Presha had called her, and Dala remembered the Biblical name meant *ornament* —her Georgia self.

"It's the *salle à manger* I've just come from, preparing their big meal—they're all big. I was tempted to shriek *hold on* when I saw you, but Garden Cliff is the least of Garden's dangers. No one has yet jumped off. Aside from overeating, it's the woods that bring most of our worries. Our faithful boxers, Sib and Gesib worry the porcupine quills. But you wouldn't believe that our most serious talent gets lost in these woods. And it's always the best mannered young man and nicest young lady together, as happened last night. I had seen them shortly after dinner talking to a visitor behind the gate. Except for appointments and the Saturday concerts *no visitors are countenanced*—Mr Betur's rule. Cars may not park inside the gate and crowd the grounds, we must keep them clear in case of fire. Well our gifted blockheads were lost circling in the woods for the night, without matches, or too scared of fire to send up flares—and mistaking our flashlights for heaven knows what. I'm responsible for the girls' curfew, and Mr Betur for the boys'. He almost had my head off. He feels so keenly for their proprieties. I could be Delilah in these mad upsets and snip his locks. But his silence becomes more punishment than I can stand when I need his advice—and I'm not allowed to proceed without it. When all lessons were postponed late this morning our lost ones turned up. They'll get the silent treatment from him for weeks. He's sick over it.

"Poor man he's sleepless in Garden—on night rounds to cabins and studios of older students—making sure all is safe. I keep telling him he should allow them *some play* in the newly built swimming pool, but afraid of accidents he insists on using it as a reservoir. As if there is not enough celery tonic, soda pop and fruit juice punch to round off the sixty gallons of milk quenching the daily hundred pounds of beef, lamb and chicken I cook in troughs whose scouring I surpervise! I run it all spic and span like a paddock in Georgia.

"You *would* think knowing how sensitive Mr Betur is, constantly urging them to sing on their instruments and drawing pure tone out of them, they'd spare him such pranks as carrying off their friends' bathroom equipment into the woods—the embarrassment of checking every night, when he can barely get himself to stutter the word in French, 'you have your *cabinet?*' I know you speak French, Little, and it is funny." (He did find it so, with propriety.) "Of course *you're* fortunate to have your own place this crowded summer. There's enough work too to do for the younger ones upstairs here, turning their beds inside out and their laundry, and seeing they write home occasionally. I have just retyped a letter for Mr Betur to a parent. I had typed *request*—but '*no,*' he says, '*I said ask.*' Wasn't he on the rock garden a moment ago? Most likely he has hurried back and is waiting anxiously for your lesson. Let me show you in."

Ada's summer talk overflowed, while Imam's remained in his mouth, except for some squibs impelled by disciplines of curriculum. Scales, exercises, pieces—his traditional rigor never wavered from his competence. Yet he was not the fool to spite his own public face and overrate a friend's or a pupil's endurance. Compassion for Presha in Pamphilia (where he needed him, he was welcome unobtrusively on Garden's Saturday Nights) evoked some musical relief, at least that summer, for his old friend's subordinate fretting over scales and exercises, and at the same time soothed Little's avidity for sightreading the repertoire that Betur sadly knew only maturity can "project" (a word the von Chulnts disliked). Without blinking at Snorckie's tacit flash of gratitude (they were two of a kind, again Verchadet saw) he would, after a surprise review of a scale or an exercise, flaunt Mozart's G major or the Mendelssohn on the music rack and say: "You like to read, READ me." While Little did Betur pencilled the fingering on the music, following the boy's most comfortable reading expeditiously. "Moch better," Betur'd say, and as Little was playing it for the first time he'd wonder why the comparative. He decided that Betur had no use for *best* and that *good* was his niggard superlative.

As Little played the boxers, who wore bells in the country so they could be heard if lost, appeared outside the uncurtained lateral French doors of the studio and listened with tilted heads. In the freedom of outdoors Betur's shooing glances could not move them away. Little noted they did not appear when other violinists played and was pleased. He sensed that Betur too was pleased, murmuring once, "Stupid, (hurts) *huts* you—from porcupines?" Little heard him express equal sympathy years later over a neuritic finger: "Oi I know it goes to the head!"

He could finger a movement of a new piece in a leisurely last fifteen minutes of a half-hour lesson, then signal its end, handing over the music with a flurry of comment: "Here, give Dr Presha, practice me good, I have my spy system." Little collected Betur's advice to others, passed on to him: "Next time don't stand like *vet* (wet) chicken.— Stand like melt'd butter—no!—Must play? no I say, work like dog(k)." He invariably refingered most of his first fingering, especially if the pupil in his practice followed him servilely, and if he had not Betur would substitute some finer difficulty, some mathematical subtlety of fingering that played even more expeditiously. Such changes were most likely after a time of letting a piece lie fallow, when the pupil least expected it, after Betur's saying "Put aside —I don't want" had seemed final. So it happened with the Mozart that summer.

Betur told Little, "The Ladies Hemdlach would appreciate if you play Mozart at Castle." Little did, but Betur did not go. Nor did Presha who might have hinted—in French —at a claim *f'r inter-prétation*. It turned out that Guy Esor Octa who was there, *spy system* Little deduced, exulted in praising thruout Pamphilia "that little one's" masterly handling of a slight slip of memory caused by the sudden distraction of sighting Mme Otototot's elephantine landscape. "Who wouldn't wander," Esor laughed.

As for the Mendelssohn there was one phrase Little bōwed after hearing Ztephiah. "Wrong(k) again!" Betur insisted, "I marked before. Mendelssohn don't want this Ztephiah bōwing, editor don't want, I don't want. How many times you want I write it, I write it *for you*. What color?" Little who admired Betur's pastel collection had one of his own. Betur had impulsively hinted at Little's markings all over his music. Unmoved but disciplined Little handed the master the faintest of yellows. The Mendelssohn was put aside.

Whether Betur's fallow concertos intended some secret *torch'r* for a future garden did not worry Little. He read. There was one piece that Betur reviewed in every lesson that summer, if only for a moment refingering his previous refingerings, paradoxically to spur Little to "R'member practice me good." When Little gently responded, "Don't worry," Betur severely retorted, "*I* say *worry*." The uncalled-for rebuke caused Little to infer that the piece was meant for his imminent Garden debut. Rumors in Pamphilia somewhat confirmed his guess. What piece more suitable than the soarings of Onangni's *Praeludium and Alle-*

gro, serious hoax of Ztirf Relsierk's own melting strings, which he had modestly attributed to the archival Onangni when audiences were all *Parsifal* and still innocent of Baroque, at least twenty-five years before Ztephiah had touched a string—so *he* would have a literature to play: Garden's musical expectants had older loyalties.

They listened to Little play Onangni behind the curtained interior French doors of Betur's summer studio, *after* Guy Esor told them of Betur's trustful prophecy for his youngest prodigy: "Comes sometime Relsierk and Ztephiah in one and knows more than they music." The most rabid cornered Little in the post office: "When are you scheduled for a public Saturday Night, Little? You will play for us won't you? We're dying to hear you." With Betur for mentor, he did not answer them. "Let them—" he would say to Verchadet and Dala and laugh when they shuddered a little disapproving his vehemence. Truthfully, the three rather expected a Garden debut. Or why had Betur without forewarning allowed Little to play the *Praeludium and Allegro* when, unexpected, Oniz Narf dropped down on Garden in his private plane. The friendly rotund Ladin virtuoso, well on in his fifties, always travelled with his youthfully vigorous mother and sometimes with his young obviously aging wife. This time they were all together. He pinched his own jowl (as Ztephiah, whose enemies said he spurned a chin rest, could never do) and then Little's cheek in praise. The mother blessed Verchadet apart: "My dear, it's *you* who will need all the strength." The wife steeled herself to a shy *au revoir.* Betur himself warmed to a muttered *very gut* as he closed the door behind the von Chulnts to celebrate with his friends.

The last three of Garden's Saturday Nights were still to be scheduled. The order of surprises turned out as the public in Pamphilia expected: Tremor would precede the greater Eichel, but the soloist of the Farewell Concert remained unannounced. Little's ambushes persisted: *they* knew *who*. The embarrassed von Chulnts replied honestly they did not know. Their ears rang with chatter. Tremor Cyclops was practicing more hours than Eichel—nowhere to be seen. Who could afford not to emulate Eichel, whose very name was Practice. No genius out of sight but gained. Did Betur believe that Little practiced only four hours a day? The von Chulnts were minimizing. Mrs Bearmeout was "distraught." She had almost been run over by Eichel in a white sports car, an elegant Triumph. He begged her not to tell his mother, frantic over his disappearances before his recital. Poor Mrs Practice the huge accompanist in tears, the thanks for her devotion.

Miss Nasaltwang true to her promise drove the von Chulnts to both solo concerts. Of Tremor's, Little had but to see the stance, the two prodigious round sweeps of the bow arm preparing as it were to wrestle with an antagonist, then the clamped hesitancy before placing the first note to know something would be lacking. He played as anyone trained by Betur played—at least visibly competent, rarely off pitch, and (if sadly it happens the heart or the head cannot keep the same pace) overwhelmed most of the audience.

Little was soon more absorbed by the circumstances. They sat on folding chairs at the rear of the grand ballroom rearranged for the concert. He knew Betur was listening at the far end of his studio, its door now open to the central stairway and entrance hall behind them. With its packed audience the ballroom was altogether too electrified, crowded for the *general* on their folding chairs and excessively comfortable for the elect sunk in sofas flanking two fireplaces that yawned to each other across the room divided by a red carpeted aisle. Drawing attention to themselves by their bells the boxers acted as ushers might, running up and down the carpet, or all the way back to Betur it would seem for instructions, infallibly skidding on several gay colored scatter rugs in the entrance hall on the return errand. The walls were mostly open leaded windows, so that

Dala struggled with the drafts all evening. Turning his neck in longing towards one sheltered corner he suddenly flinched self-conscious under the meaningless gaze of the smiling Ira Taignit. Tho Little did not expect attention from Betur during the intermission, he could not help noticing the ceremoniousness with which the teacher he thought of as reserved kissed the hands of the Hemdlach sisters, the cheek of Mme Otototot; the courtesy of conversation extended to Mr and Mrs Cyclops seemed far in excess of the casual nod to his parents. The ceremoniousness at Eichel's concert was even more extravagant—Betur a gallant European kissing Mrs Practice regaled in diamonds.

As Dala's most devious reflection might put it, the enthusiasm of the audience was as affectively as it was infectiously unanimous, no omniscient observer who had not become nescient. Eichel had whipped thru several styles of two hundred years of violin literature in forty minutes, allowing his admirers to breathe only their gasping praises. To Little, despite the impressive facility, all of it had sounded as tho it went nowhere, except for one Paganini caprice. Its unstalled brilliance, the leaps of the most sensitive racehorse, had been endangered by too much cherishing, too much currying. The same horse plodded thru the encore, a fluff of songs "my mother taught me" preceded by his softly spoken homage. "It's no compliment, Verch," Little whispered. "To me it wouldn't be." Only her lips spoke. The boy tried to wink one eye at her, but inevitably both eyes winked, and he looked down to avoid a chuckle. In the shuffle of everybody rising "I doubt—" she started to say to Dala, and stepping into the night on the way to Miss Nasaltwang's sedan—Miss N was still chatting with Eichel—"I am sure Betur has cancelled Little's Garden debut for this summer." "What did you say?" Little who was walking adventurously ahead called back. "Nothing," Baballo said, "just that the headlights of these cars cast shadows, it's hard to see what is level." "Follow me," Little called back again, "or you'll be lost in Ada's woods."

Verchadet's firm doubt proved right. When the triad arrived at the entrance hall for the summer's final lesson they stopped to read an announcement of the Farewell Concert: a septet with Ambrose Flutit as pianist. They showed no concern sitting in their usual chairs as Little tuned. Again Betur asked for the *Praeludium and Allegro*. With no show of anger, Little played it at a speed that they sensed almost caused Betur to gasp. In the last wisp of bravura the bow masterfully poised above the strings flew out of his fingers across the room. The three laughed spontaneously. "Don't laugh, no laughs at concert," Betur reproved them, while cosmopolites they detected he smiled like a bedbug who seems pleased.

20

Summer's end was celebrated in Garden with an annual Farewell Masquerade Ball. On Betur's part it was a lingering *fête galante*—a courtesy to those of Garden's patrons who, after the Farewell Concert, did not flee Pamphilia at once to their autumn ways. To Little's second sight it was perhaps a way of saying in behalf of ambushes and musical followers, *Lest we forget*. Not that the ambushes needed a reminder. Not to miss a trick they would have stretched awake to the shining dark on Garden's grounds until the first frost, when the studio and dining hall were shut down and boarded for the winter. But it was the *manth* (month) he wanted loneliness for his rock garden, or Ada tacitly following advice, or a mute over a bourbon. *"E-noff* (enough) *student'* (students), they come more than I want in October." The only breaks into his vacation would be a lesson forced on him by his fears over Eichel's lack of interest in an early fall recital, and two free lessons he would give to the marine band boy on furlough. Jon the marine: his violinist's life had been interrupted by a summons to military service. Betur's dedication to the precious violin as instrument of worldly culture—he had no opinions on political illegality or war—was sufficient reason to sacrifice some hours of his vacation. "How's bugle?" "Fine, sir—easy." "Mm . . . for *that* one study *nineteen* years violin . . ."

Distantly, perhaps because he was farsighted, he would then look at Jon's uniform with compassion equal to that for his boxers smarting from porcupine quills.

Miss Nasaltwang in ethnic costume drove the von Chulnts to the Ball. Summer's lease a week to run out, Mrs Watherbureau's forecast fair, they too longed for "a little vacation," Snorckie for adventure, for some fun that seemed likely after the letdown of no debut had estranged all the curious, none of them working. He was masked as Hammurabi in an old satin dress of Verchadet, so that he moved like a short block of black diorite as he imagined it moving by some mechanism out of his ancient history book. On or about his chest pinned by a tiny safety pin was THE CODE in white on a small oblong card framed under cellophane. "Always ingenious," Miss Nasaltwang spired rising after bending and failing to read it without her glasses. Verchadet and Dala had not thought of costumes for themselves—ready, she said, if they were required at the ballroom doors, to say that the summer in Garden had already disguised them. They went chiefly to be with Little, or as her doubt led her to feel for no other reasonable reason. Maybe the reason will clarify, Dala considered—anticipating one or another quick retort for her to as many offenders.

No one embarrassed their arrival, nor was it greeted. A string ensemble of the literally handicapped—Betur's gift over successive summers of the violin to the cure of muscular dystrophy—was playing fervently: backed, perhaps for resonance, along one wall by stacks of folded chairs that only last week had filled the dance floor. It had been cleared, and of the not more than two dozen who had come to the Ball each one wandered rather sparsely in her (or his) costume, the masks eminently recognizable. They were: Tremor as the great Bach; Panza as Verdi; Lona as La Bohème (da Leoncavallo); Marj as Constanze; May as Frau von Bülow; the boy Japanese cellist Nogo as Washington crossing the Delaware; etc—that is, a few strangers.

Eichel was not there, but no one who was saw anything recognizable in Snorckie's dress as he walked among them stiffly—he preferred not to smile in public. Jon the marine came in uniform. First, Jon danced with Marj, while Tremor watched them and imitated their dance with Panza; then May danced with Jon, while Panza watched them and imitated their dance with Tremor; then Constanze danced with Jon, while Frau von Bülow, Tremor and Panza watched; then Jon danced with Frau von Bülow, while Constanze, Panza and Tremor danced together; then Verdi, Bach and Lona *La Bohème da* Leoncavallo, Marj, May and Jon the marine who had not missed a partner for a second, and the strangers who had not danced joined in a square dance, while Miss Nasaltwang, not inclined, danced with little Nogo, "Washington crossing the Delaware."

Betur looked up at them from his hand, Gesib at his feet, rarely speaking between hands of his card game with Esor Octa in a pillowed window seat, and Little wandered over to pat her. His teacher did not notice him at first—distantly conscious that the parents had been sitting, silent as usual, patiently waiting for his youngest prodigy in the adjacent window seat. "Unzung gone back to Turkey," Little overheard his considered speech. After a longish pause, he reminisced: "Rogerg, Rogerg Yksrogi"—the Apollonic bass viol one historian of music called him, Esor's great predecessor at Garden—"no one beat me at cards, only once Rogerg, I let him, and he could play—also poker." He glanced down sideways at Gesib and saw Little. "Enjoying?" he asked. "Why Liszt?" he said inferring the abbé from Little's costume. "What does card—badge—say?" Snorckie looked puzzled: "Not Liszt, THE CODE—of Hammurabi." "Ah-há," Betur said, tho THE CODE, while he played his hand, meant less than Hammurabi to the later line of Assur.

Verchadet and Dala rose to tell Little perhaps he ought

not disturb Mr Betur. "Not 't all," he said having heard them, still looking at his cards, and in afterthought, "this dŏz (does) it"—the round, the game his, he leaned in a mere gesture of moving the stakes—a tray of shelled almonds on an end table—closer to himself. "*Moany* (money) no option, gambling not for students"—and in fact his example to them was always exemplary—"if you have the merchandise, *they* come, customers come, not *fest* (fast) may be, but *they* come." Verchadet heard herself having said it after she said it, "It must be trying tho, Mr Betur, for a fast horse in reserve, waiting for ten slow horses to come in first." The slight nearly avoided wrinkle in his forehead showed her he felt her sally, a delayed droll wording like his. Yet his ears did not seem to hear. He understood but did not honor this lady who might be a compatriot. "Not mŏch refreshment tonight. *Pliz* (please)" he coaxed the von Chulnts, "Cake?"

He had seen Ada and Sib approaching with a mocha layer. "I am so sorry," she said to the von Chulnts. "Once school closes and the lessons stop, Mr Betur and I don't go in for heavy cooking. But there is punch in the dining hall, the dancers alas have consumed the pop. I did make and expected ice cream, only it seems to be warming the refrigerators. Calamity on top of drudgery in the kitchen, you know. Maybe the setting will adjust itself if we give it a chance and talk for a while in that window seat—it looks so lonesome empty. Let us spare the men." The parents returned to their seat with her, Little stayed with the men.

Dala felt obligated to chat, "I haven't seen Dr Presha around. Didn't he come?" "O," said Ada, "Blume takes him right back to the city after the lessons end. Dear Carmen, she has her singing lessons when the summer movie here closes." He had no prepared reply, and felt as tho he himself had come out of a bad movie.

"Have you had a good vacation?" Ada asked Verchadet. "As a matter of fact," Verchadet said, "I find it unpleasant living in other people's houses and our place in Pamphilia is exposed to the street." "I know how it is when one is used to one's own, I hope you hadn't too much to clean up, we've had our skirmishes with Croton bugs, but you must learn to *protect* yourself," Ada stressed proverbially, "tho as you know in Georgia we're usually hospitable. The first summer here is the hardest. To those who must return to Garden year after year the sublets are second homes." "Until now," Verchadet revealed thoughtlessly, "we've travelled to different places every summer." "O but what about Little—when one has a prodigy on hand—" it was all too obvious for Ada to say more. "I should think a vacation," Verchadet's answer followed, "would make him play better." At once modest and sure as to her "merchandise," Verchadet meant her concern was his health—it was enough for a mother that he drove his own genius. Dala's gloom dispelled by her answer upheld her, tho he did not see where it would lead her with Ada. "O but for violinists it doesn't work that way, why even Practice," Ada honored Eichel with his family name, "comes back regularly to Mr Betur for lessons. By the way," she quickened, "the Castle estate is to let next summer. If you're interested I can phone the caretaker, it might help." "Everything is possible," Dala said not knowing what he was saying, but certain that Verchadet's mind was this very moment intent on rock wall and castle across the highway from their present shambles. They had been returning the caretaker's greetings on their daily way back from the post office, had even chatted. The coincidence of Ada referring to him moved Verchadet like all coincidences that in themselves are pleasant. Despite her doubt, if she let Dala explain it to her philosophically (which she would not care to have him do) she *entertained* probability if she let it be possible. She was always better at figures than Dala. "Why, yes," she said to Ada, "thank you if you will speak for us. Half a choice is better than one since it offers two." Ada not sure of their minds said, "Will do."

Sparser in far corners of the ballroom the tired dancers were playing cards. Esor joined one group after another. Betur, apparently content to be left alone with Little, thought back vaguely—"What card—badge—say? ah-yes —THE CUD. I can *shedule* you," he said holding his head, "*wance* (once) a week lessons back in city in October. Dr Presha maybe not necessary for you next year, has too mŏch to do, tell *y'māther* I tell him. Next year in Garden, Wizard—Endor—come hear *you*." He had not mentioned Dala, perhaps an oversight, but Little said nothing, obviously gratified. "Good-bá, practice me good." Little shook hands: "Good-bye." "Wait," Betur said, "maybe soup ice cream ready." But Miss Nasaltwang was anxious to go; they were all "leaving Pamphilia the day after tomorrow, *au revoir*."

"I almost told Miss Nasaltwang," Baballo said. "What vanity," said Verchadet. They stayed up half that night bubbling, so to speak, over their fortune by themselves. "What vanity," Little added, "it's good you didn't." "Are you sure Betur said what you said about Endor?" Verchadet asked to confirm it to herself. "Tell me again," Little said, "how Dala nearly spoiled it with Ada about the castle." "Dr Presha will probably feel hurt," Dala said. "He's not your assistant, but Betur's," Little scored, "*that* takes care of that. When will you stop taking care of the world?" "One concentrated lesson a week will be simpler for me," Verchadet said, but her fair enough reason did not clarify. He went off to write in his notebook—'in two removed window seats by telesthesia—' "Well, Little you'd prefer a castle to this hovel, if—" Verchadet said. "A hostel hovel," Little spelled it out for her on paper. "It's late," Dala yawned, "one more day here, tomorrow the caretaker."

They met him at noon the next day—no last letters, no

one at the post office. "I've watched you across the highway," he said, "and I know you won't bother me and I won't bother you." A deposit, returnable if they changed their minds before next June, would hold it for them. "Do you have the return train tickets?" Little asked Verchadet as he looked over the amount on Dala's check. "The boy knows his business," the caretaker laughed. "Come here, let me show you a bit, I'd show you all of it, only the young folk are coming for their lawn party later this afternoon. Twenty-four rooms!" They were convinced by a glimpse of the grand stairway, but Little by this time was coming out of the nearest room. "A library!" was all he said. "We have to pack for home," said Verchadet, "we can see it all next year." They were out on the terrace again. "A greenhouse?" she asked. "Used to be," said the caretaker, "that's where they throw out their furniture. They'll probably have me empty it for the bonfire tonight."

She stood at the door of the glass structure and saw a few dead plants and roots thrust thru heaps of furniture. "What a lovely little spindle-back hickory chair," she said. "They'll probably burn it," the caretaker said. "Burn it? O no!" "Could be used for violin practice?" Snorckie referred to the greenhouse. "Suit yourself," the caretaker said, and spoke again to Verchadet: "Come to think of it, there are three of those chairs—one for each of you—let me crate and send them to you for Christmas, they'll never miss them." He appeared enriched when she gave him a little more than the freight charges.

Meanwhile Dala and Little had walked on to the woods and mountain behind the house. The pine needles that looked as tho they might kindle under them sank cool and soft underfoot as they entered the edge of woods. They rose tall with the mountain. Dala's nostrils whiffed a few short breaths of pine odors. "We'll climb it next year," he said. "Aye," Little said, "with my coonskin hat?"

Droves of the Castle clan filled the lawn towards evening. The lessees of next summer watched tense from across the highway. About midnight the voices reaching them grew louder. The bonfire roared. When the fieldstone walls darkened safely, the von Chulnts went to bed.

21

Now Betur was his only teacher Little rebuffed the faults of his own practice to spare Betur the trouble. Eight years old that year in taking pains he would say: "Little Baron Snorck, to yourself." Like most people with their own names that suggest a lot is doing, he expected courtesy everywhere, tho he despised the flattery of showing courtesy to everyone. One fall day Dala in an engrossed walk back and forth behind the closed doors of the largest room in his brownstone—wanting to say good-bye before leaving for the Institute but not wanting to disturb his son—overheard three voices. In the past, his good-bye held back by the same scruple, he had often heard only one voice: Little's to itself. But now, tho he was sure Little was alone, he heard three.

"Signore Paganini, that son of—your Nicolo won't keep time, squeaks when he shifts; his A-string the treble of a tinny Signorina Verona Moronica; the G—a German howler raising haunches into his shoulders." "O Professore Betur, let Césare judge—O Caesar, *pian pianino!*" "That little one failing me? No! how? He has extended me superlative contributions, great favors of dedicated compositions; if you don't approve, Professore, why do you teach him? He must never be cowed into what *you* call strenuous practice."

He was never cowed, requiting Betur with more than his due in competence. Yet his musicality, Little's strictly personal gift to himself, craved to be heard in Great Hall. Betur's promise that "Wizard" (he had meant Warlock) would hear him in Garden next year reminded Little of Warlock's earlier promise: "You must play for me again in six months, and the third time will be in Great Hall." Little forgot in modest homage to Little and fiddle that six months had lagged into twice six. As Dala *pithed it* (an expression Little discovered for him): work drives beyond promise, craving and time. Perhaps Verchadet recalled—and not too surely—the chilling words Betur meant for Dala but addressed to her when they had first called on him: "You see, I don't prepare anyone for a debut. I just teach." As tho Betur now encouraged her to forget that first puff of disavowal and last summer's proof of it in Garden, he startled the von Chulnts by telephoning one evening after lessons: "Miz von Chulnt? A lady *colt* me"—*called* me, Verchadet half realized. "Name, Osmir Nishgood, sorority of Chiromeles"—all spelled out. "Would like musicale entertainment like *Ladies of Yesteryear* she explained me. I recommend Little, she very pleased. Could prepare his own program. I trost him."

Like Betur, Little took *trust* to mean a bond for "merchandise" to be delivered. "It won't do," he badgered Verchadet, "to give them what they've been getting from Tremor and Eichel. I'm sick of Onangni and the Cochon *Quicksand Concerto* with piano score, where you'll be sure to end up two measures behind me—that's for privacy with Betur." "But if he hasn't heard you play the pieces, do you think he'll like *Daring Do*," Verchadet worried, "when he hears about it?" "I don't care, he said he trusts me. Besides he will probably be assigning it to Eichel and Tremor to *practice me good* once I've premiered it," Little said with finality. "No Bach for violin alone, no, no Mozart—they won't listen. What do you think, Verchadet—an untranscribed seventeenth-century English piece or some early American—something for fiddle to sound like a French horn, never heard before?" The Chiromeles, most of them ancient widows and second wives of retired garden farmers and fishermen in the export business at Sheepshead, an inlet of the sea some miles from the von Chulnts' brownstone, must have their cheated tastes revived and spiced for the true violin literature, Little argued. "You mean," Dala interrupted almost unheard, "they're—sort of—country people and seafolk, once high class, bored by a century of concert going so they cannot stir to how near the true classic is to work in progress?" "Yeh—yeh—" Little sidestepped, "they've had enough vespers, leit motives, chorale *gehag te lieber Gott*, cantata *ah soul, o test, how cool the*—in organ versions of Beer Hand Baer after grand voluntaries of Tusk O'Ninny—but if you're hinting at modern kitten music by L. O. Quint and Lapping Furtive, DON'T HINT, please." Dala did not answer. At their age the Sheepshead ladies would probably not hold Little responsible for his father's scholarly eyeglasses, if they saw thru their own bifocals. Good—Little obviously required his own research.

The von Chulnts went to the Library. Little perched on a high oak stool over an oak table in the vaulted catalog room, of an age for all the world like the daguerreotype of The Old Librarian, tho without Franklin's spectacles, filling out slips for books and scores, while Dala with his new uncomfortable rimless glasses carted the index trays to him. Verchadet waited at a table in the communing reading room for the arrivals of Little's choice from the vaults of the vast interior. By the time the three gathered at her table for Little to make his selection the music had piled up higher than her head, and the other nearby readers who slept or pored or merely observed were roused to an educated if unworldly family. "Drayhorse," Little whispered as he caught Dala drowsing, "sorry, don't nod, I'll be thru soon—here's a lullaby for piano—if you'd like to copy it out for me?"

Research became a fair portion of Little's winter work or public disappearances, as he worded it shyly to a colleague, a little girl at the music school who had asked him where he had been some previous Saturdays. For his history the Chiromeles concert went well enough. There were other performing engagements that year: *youth concerts* taking him to provincial watering places, as a wry critic described them, annoyed perhaps by young audiences slaking their thirst around the drinking fountains near the wash rooms when *he* was trying to listen and praise a virtuoso of *their* time. "I don't mind," Little said to this critic, "*de gustibus*—just don't give over half of your review to *them*." For all the praise and friendly crowding over the signing of autographs—Little varied these, sometimes his first name, sometimes his last, sometimes *von*—these engagements never brought him a return engagement. Baffled by this result Verchadet explained to herself that Little's fleeting admirers, even the old Chiromeles strove like her son to be original each year in their selection of entertainment.

Behind Little's public appearances she always sensed Betur's permission. Why he gave it she could not guess, except maybe to strengthen practice with audiences. Uncommitted—"They ask," he'd say, "so if you like, good luck." How could she refuse an impartial wish? Fortunately the engagements occurred on week-ends, when Dala not obliged to his Institute could help carry three small valises, one for each of them—their insides mostly Little's belongings. The fiddle case was *Défense de toucher,* the soloist warned them, for him to carry himself, and at intervals his to unlock to tune the fiddle as they travelled.

The weather's *fair*
the teeth ache

the weather *changes*
the teeth ache

the weather's *the weather*
the teeth ache

Despite himself the verses sluiced thru Dala's head. With clinched fists, "Be quiet both of you," Little muttered, "if you don't keep quiet I promise you'll never again travel with me to my concerts."

They sat on their made beds in a room of a fashionable last century hotel in the nation's capital after reading the morning paper's review which Little had run downstairs to bring up to them. The reviewer of his appearance as soloist the night before with The Symphonia had praised Little and taken away. Rereading they hurt with ire for him. "In the tuttis the flying brilliance of the soloist's half-size was understandably but regrettably obscured"—Dala strained at the duplicity of the words. "Who cares!" Little flared up again, "maybe he's saying *cows brayed*!" "They did," Verchadet said, "I've never been deafened by a worse orchestra —o QUIET, both of you." Little saw his father hesitating towards a leaf of hotel stationery: "Don't dare, don't dare, Dala, write the fool or whoever a protesting letter!" The doorbell rang and to Verchadet who answered it appeared a bouquet of American Beauties, so many with a tag wired into them reading *For Little von Chulnt from The Manager.* "O thank you, how lovely," Verchadet said only to realize the bellboy had gone. "I must ask the maid for a vase for these." The roses went with her as she shut the door.

"Father Peremptore," Dala said looking down into his son's eyes. "I say what I mean," Little flustered, "don't dare write for me—and if ever in fiction, to spare me, condense. What were you doing with that scrap of waste paper?"

"Welshing," Dala said.

"Before or after the review," Little teased.

"Last night," Dala said.

Little stalked over, leaned his waist to read standing, his chin in his palms, elbows on the table:

> not o' wame a' that
> Pan hymn $D\bar{\imath}$ go not
> am cry am create
> o Nine wreathe 'll laugh & knot
> o fruit of fruit thew
> o fruit to deck or root
> o really a blood hue brae
> o flight gie to goad dew
> o preed o preed rath
> Pan hymn $D\bar{\imath}$ go not
> o flight down at
> o dew veer to nine wet

"Taliesin?" Little asked.

"Well, yes," Dala answered, "for my purpose he'll do. You open your mouth sounding off, but sometimes you close it." With the reviewer in mind he said: "I too have been charged with obscurity, tho it's a case of listeners wanting to know too much about me, more than the words say."

"You know me," Little said matter-of-fact and unrepentant: Verchadet had just come back with a vase.

23

Concrete poetry—a hundred years ago it was marble—Dala mulled over a late magazine, I hope my teeth qualify. He mulled further: to be sure is to be unsure, and to be unsure is to be sure? that one's matter in history or out of it was "work," "a useless work," "a fine work," "Square's works," "ZZZ's works," "Etc's." Has not Verchadet said, 'Who hasn't worked, for the rich to dress in the morning was work.'

Also work the pleasures of their concert trips were chiefly historical. Travelling southerly to Little's concert at a Moravian counterpart of Garden, they visited Dala's old friend R. Z. Draykup who had been confined to a madhouse. As he put it, 'he hath spoke sooth'—and for Dala these archaic words completely expressed the sorrow of his friend's incarceration. In time he would be released, but not cleared of the charge of madness implying a sanity for which he had risked being executed. He would never be pardoned for the compassion which inflamed him into raving speech against "gall, vices and lackeys" somehow involved in medieval echoes most modern folk heard as "Gulf whites and gibbet blacks." For him Little played Bach *for violin alone* with results which the concrete reader may, if he can rove while gazing solidly, read as another chapter. For the time being, during this stop Little confided to Draykup that a concert tour involved being the fodder of audiences. "Ah, but you're a performer," Draykup took exception, "Ewe hev to fader"—and he spelled it out on paper for him, much as Little himself might have.

With the Deep South Symphony Little played Mozart's G major for the youth in the afternoon and the mature in the evening. The lady of Welsh lineage Lledil who introduced both occasions effervesced, "What pretty tunes!" But —apparently stone deaf—she only looked straight at him when he asked after the girl, about his own age, in the lilac dress who had helped serve the afternoon tea. He had *thought*, he said, her black skin with her blue eyes and kinky red hair *unusually* beautiful.

James Madison, who aging had been ailing, wrote about that time pleading for news of Little's musical engagements and themselves, and Dala wrote her about two other appearances:

> I am still terrified when Little stands at the edge of his own three-foot square platform, which the conductors always need to overcome the battery of the orchestra behind the solo part, that he will fly up on an upbow and fall off. In The University Hall, looking away from him all the time, I sat in an acoustically dead spot, and when the concerto ended I hurried frantically to Verchadet to ask what had happened. "He played well, that's all," she said. Later we were taken to a colonial brick mansion furnished entirely with antiques—the conductor's residence, apparently open house to everybody any time of day. The uninvited guests serve themselves out of two stocked refrigerators. They may also handle anything on the property. Little did, running upstairs and down to come up to tell us that in the basement music room (the mansion has three music rooms) was Haydn's own clavichord and a replica of Bach's. Simply there they were: wood keys, boxwood painted green.

We finally got him to go to the train where he found the railroad's vice-president to talk to across the aisle—who said it was a pleasure—while I dozed off with pain in my right eye, not having dared to infringe on the refrigerators, which tho free for anybody to open, as I saw, would after all shut.

Easter, in Neufafen Little received a check of $50 and took us out. He spent $14.32 for fare, coffee, milk and hot cross buns, but not a penny more: Bach himself when it comes to economy. Verchadet risking not too obviously to implant generosity hinted he make it a straight 15, but he wouldn't hear of it. Guess I had better go back to my *Bards* and maybe earn $29.50 in three years—and forget the drafty trains that other passengers find comfortable. Little has now read me the praise in The Neufafen Journal-Currier, gloating over the spelling "Mazas" for Mozart—the point being one of his earliest student étude books is by Mazas. A cold wind's in my overcoat.

Affectionately

A tang of next fall, was it, in April? Not Little, but Verchadet and Dala lived their past sometimes into the future: the
annual gathering of their families on Little's birthday had
been delayed by his public disappearances at the turn of
the year. With grandpa gone Little did not want to see family, but he could still be persuaded. "Every year it has been
the same bickering—you'd think—" Verchadet began the
midnight before their visit, when Dala in perspective broke
in: "The loneliness of the artist—the loneliness of a da
Vinci, no forbears tho there were forbears—yet we live to a
convergence, of it with our kin."

For the third time in three years Little arrived without
his fiddle. *"Enough"*—the families had heard his first
notes, when something to talk about and hail, as any lazy
public might say reflecting pride on itself, *for them* he had
"arrived." The ever embedded Count and the complaining
Contessa—her antiques more dingy in shining from constant polishing—did not remember to ask after the fiddle,
nor did the others—the younger Esfelts and the older Lucy
and Hiram. They were more interested in the travels of the
von Chulnts as tho, Verchadet suspected, they—not the von
Chulnts—had been deprived of confidence in their worldly
attainments. Not that Verchadet wanted to disenchant them
of what they thought glamorous. *Their* disillusion would

give *her* no comfort. Little stood off. Dala swallowed his obligatory burden, feeling less obliged to their envy—tho he could not believe it—in silence. But Verchadet showed her pleasure in the verbal flight of the Count who—when Tearilee with a shiver of her slight shoulders and a pious wish in her hazel eyes said, "Cold today—where's spring?" —whispered in his bedding, "Behind." Verchadet let his one word speak for her too, what good would it do to tell them: Little has played in many cold places; invariably with a cold that hung on tho he had to play warm; over the air without a proscenium before phantoms; for a microphone affording no greater fidelity than a hi-fi; with a string workshop so he could encourage the sloths and in innocence help a famous old lady cellist who coached them keep a job; had, during a year of Mozart celebrations, reenacted (three times) the legend of little Mozart (with ruches trimming gold crewelworked aquamarine velveteen) replacing the first violinist the first time Leopold let his son play with a grown-up quartet, so that an actual first violinist forty years old would begrudge Little the indignity for life; and furthered the Triennial Festival of Recent Composers, only to be chagrined by the dean of critics who, extolling Little for his performance of the work dedicated to him, neglected to mention the name of the composer along with the others who made up the program, all lumped as a "pride" (mere lions) "from whom Little had stolen the show." And if these affronts were due to Betur's attentions where was the glamor?

Saying good-bye at the door the young Count grown more portly not knowing what to say spoke as older cousin: "Keep your chin up." Looking up at six foot-three Little replied, "A fiddle doesn't need a butler for that." And when grandma Tearilee said to him, "You look *so art*"—an expression which held for her all the aspiration for the extraordinary she naturally felt but which somehow could never be close to her—Little said, "Thank you."

Still spring vacation the day after, Dala went with Little for his lesson with Betur while Verchadet tended the hyacinth bulbs in her garden. "Here *pater pote*, you may brood the last page while I have my workout," Little said leaving him with his "dairy." Dala read:

> Courtesy whin do'n' dee wére nighed
> courtesy dear handed me I'm all eyed
> courtesy dire a feather, I vied
> high I see been pour eye gimp again guide
> courtesy chock have a' th' pech, hide—
> when glare irk when garret him dare hide
> courtesy sigh'th ai if quiet gored 'n' gnawed
> courtesy within hall pith path or wider gained
>   is the deigned rock towered

Happy with the brood of words he still looked at Dala heard himself thinking, "May soon." "Lucky I was reminded," he said aloud, leaving his check for the caretaker of the Castle in Pamphilia in the diary and closing it. "Might be *Gorhoffedd*," Dala said returning the diary to Little who had brisked up with a scowl and closed fiddle case. "What's this," he asked. "Chock," Dala said, "remind me to mail it." Little shut both eyes several times in winking them.

26

A gait   an unhurried   eat gear hastened—

translated the lessee of the Castle walked grateful to be
alive in June to a different vacation in Pamphilia, last
year's out of mind. Sunlight shed a pearl's luster on him
from the twenty-four long windows of his leasehold, the
length of a city block to the kitchen. He was up earlier than
Little, to rake the embers of the wood fire in the cast iron
oven he had assured the night before and to make breakfast
where the three would be warmed by risen sun and kindled
log. Beyond hearing him Verchadet and Little slept on
under six counterpanes, each in an oak paneled bedroom
with its door to the library: Little clasping *The Mabinogion*
he had pried from the tallest (lowest) shelf of the Lieutenant Governor's unused collection. The violinist's bow hand
strained to its fretted place at the end of *Manawyddan the
Son of Llyr*, third of the four-branch tale of the Mabinogi.
But Dala for their waking toasted white dough to a coppery
tinge on aluminum foil, wrapped the crisp rolls in it, and
when they were diapered placed them with the intent of his
absent mind into the still spotlessly clean antique tole pail
reserved for newspapers for the fire. Until now pine bark
had served. Abruptly untranslated by his error he dis-
carded the foil and removed the rolls to the oak dining
table where a slab of board incised with the word BREAD

awaited them: the board's underside similarly encouraged BUTTER. So as the three ate Dala sheepishly had a tale to tell on himself, not unlike the knight Kynon to his own discredit in the "The Lady of the Fountain," the ninth tale of the Mabinogi Little would read this morning. Not uproariously—they laughed.

"Let well alone enough," Little inverted and Verchadet decided against Dala's and her own craving for the rare thing sometimes lost in an attic. After one cobwebby inspection by all three together they agreed for their sensible needs to sublet the upper stories of the Castle to mystery. Betur had definitely scheduled Little's performance of *Praeludium and Allegro* for the Farewell Concert in August, and Little's precise musical runs anticipating Warlock listening deterred Dala from climbing stairs to some blurred confusion like—'Is it Warlock or Wizard cum Endor—well, let August tell.' It was pleasant to listen, a solitary on the terrace, and the distracting birds were welcome. So, Dala had no doubt, Mrs Weatherbureau across the highway also listened to Little practicing in the greenhouse. Let us enjoy the grounds, the terrace and the main floor, the three agreed, and of its eleven rooms leave three with their silver, stoneware and crystal untouched except for an occasional brightening with feather-duster or dry-mop on the way to the kitchen. Country dust is not dirt. And let us not use the outdoor grate to cook on. Mrs Otototot was overheard whispering to them in the post office: "my—where have you kept yourselves, your rent must be enormous." Few visitors crossed their private bridge. Lambeth Potiphar, in confidence "by herself," on a brief excursion from Turkey came to call Unzung long distance and found the von Chulnts' telephone disconnected. Esor Leber saying he was "driven by family"—Verchadet and Dala had not heard or seen the station wagon—invited himself to the greenhouse for practice before Little could "warm" them with a surprised *n-no!* Some hours' rumbles of runs and intervals on the bass viol justified Little's claim to the greenhouse. His parents glared not exactly at each other while he smiled at them chasing himself from one room to another, out to the terrace and in again. Verchadet's migraine commiserated with her geraniums behind the glass walls accustomed to gentler vibrations. Dala immersed himself in *Timon of Athens*, moved as always by it, between recurrences of queasiness. Their release arrived when, expecting to be coaxed to come again, Esor thanked them profusely. Intending a friendly good-bye thru his pallor, Dala said "what for" and suddenly faint but still smiling went on, "I reread it over your bass," pointing to the spine of *Timon*. Esor, quick to analyse others, left abruptly, looking as tho he could never brook a neurotic competitor. "I should've—" Dala gasped, as Verchadet and Little seated him in an armchair to his discomfort, and then resolved more firmly, "had he stayed a minute longer I'd have invited him to lunch." Little was more explicit: "I am hungry too, that's what's the matter with you." On the whole the status or situs of the Castle precluded visitors. Budgeted but not conscious of budgeting they never regretted renting the Castle.

There was romance that summer for Verchadet when her yellow dry-mop swept from her floor brilliant petals and blown anthers fallen from bouquets she renewed daily, and for Little and Dala there was adventure. When they sought it they incurred differences of weather without its being forecast: when they sauntered in hot sun, or raced in cold brake, then bathed under the bridge, feet and legs timid on sharp rock in the trout brook called The Breath the first dip literally carried the breath away. In the late afternoon, the sun still high Little renamed it The Midges, so pestiferous were "these things" flying in the face of the sun. They were not certain when a cloud over the woods shadowing their meadow might as at will shut out the sun from the Castle. What Pamphilians called *high fog* was not rare. But last year's promise to themselves to climb the mountain they carried out on a day when the blue of the sky was the sun's alone. Perspired (against Verchadet's wishes if she were there) on the warm comforter of pine needles at the edge of woods—their red sagging fired Little and Dala into them: the woods chilled them, they climbed.

"And what a climb," Little reported to Verchadet, "a miracle we've come back with eyes! We couldn't find the path up—so it was over rocks and thru bramble, with the trees to hold onto. What we mistook for a path was usually smooth rock which slid us into other tangles. Branches we held back for each other to crawl under, Indian file, snapped back vice versa." "I don't suppose you had time to say face to face you were sorry," Verchadet said, slightly queasy over their recklessness—"or congratulate each other on not tearing your trousers?" Little chortled, but did not interrupt his story for her: "Craziest thing, there *was a path* a few yards around from the rock where we started— the path we came back on. Climbing we must have skirted it all the time, while looking for a clearing ahead or blue sky above that turned out to be blue spruce until we crawled out at the top into a meadow." At his mentioning blue spruce, *"Those* I'm sorry to have missed." Verchadet said. "Dala might from the start have hung his glasses on a twig—the twigs always angled for them, like the branch for Absalom." A casual look and smile expressed Dala's thanks for his son's use of The Old Testament once read to him. "Coming down took very little time," Dala added by way of apology for the worry their longish absence had brought her, "only I was more winded." "Did you find a horse," Verchadet said to recall to him the one occasion he rode one and "experienced his ribs in his heart." "Are you all right now?" she asked quietly.

They had not told her what they said and saw when they crawled out on the meadow at the top: perhaps because they knew that she had their very same talk on her mind gathering her bouquets for the Castle that summer, and flowers curtailed her speaking of lesser lives not so pretty or candid or magnificent; or perhaps because Little who confided in both his parents preferred not to place his secrets all at once in one basket so to speak and staggered them, often to V, less often to D, but quite sure he'd find them in the long run in one basket in any case—why deprive himself of the pleasure of showing up either one caught red-handed as having blabbed to the other? The top of the mountain received Little and Dala gasping near Indian Reservation they had visited with Verchadet a year ago by car at less hazard. It led them to where the musical doctors, dentists, artists and writers lived—Little's last summer's ambushes. On the road circling the meadow was Serp's place still boarded. "Serp, Lona's teacher—you remember, Dala—Betur's rival who once taught Nihunem, tho Lona is his last pupil." "Poor Lona, we wish her well," Dala said out of personal wistfulness. "Like Manawyddan, whose story you read last night, tho we try hard someone is always pushing us out of a livelihood, or could it be *we* are a bit envious." "No," Little said, "it's just that we strike them so sure and don't bother them for false sympathy like they do us that makes them hate us. So like the thievish boors or bad craftsmen whom Manawyddan's competence infuriated they'd kill us. And I'd just as soon kill them first." "Not so," Dala said, "we will not *slay* them—take it in the new or in the old sense—as Manawyddan said, *if need be do our work elsewhere.*" "Then let's get back to Castle and Verchadet fast," said Little, and they did. And tho he had forgotten to bring his coonskin hat from the city—or secretly felt too old to bring it—he bounded down as if he wore it, protected from falling boughs and all dastardly reservations.

The fiddle of sprucewood was fortunate. Hoarfrost on yellow petal in mid-August dawn, followed by cold and clear, token of more frost the night of Little's debut at Garden, protected the bouts from humidity. There is always the risk of the bouts' minutest splitting, "when the fiddle moss go to th' o'pital"—there was no hospital for fiddles in Garden—Betur was used to stammer before enunciating, "then it plays *too* open, *too* resounding." But with his music in mind, tuning occasionally was all the worry Little spared himself the long day before the concert. He was to play last, after an evening of Flutit and Esor. "It's the waiting that's dullest," Verchadet whispered. Dala could not hear her or the bass under the blunt thud of Flutit's piano. They stood in Betur's studio, all the interior doors of the ground floor of the main house open, looking beyond the entrance hall into the concert room. When the crowd separated them by an arm's length Dala saw her as in a gap between them thru a mist of Welsh sorcery. The playing stopped: he heard fainthearted applause, and while it thinned, hurried worried Betur—was turning, examining Little's fiddle, belly, bouts, back, furlings, tailpiece, pegs—retreated to a corner. From there Little was to walk down the length of carpet, the boxers having anticipated him jangling their bells on their collars, to his two-and-a-half-foot cube of platform. Dala glimpsed Little in possession of his fiddle, but waited till he was well out of the corner before edging to replace him in it. And there, standing or in their seats, were the peers straining to look at the fiddle, all the eyes the von Chulnts had avoided that summer alone in their castle: Panza Rilty, Schwerscheide, Lona, Solo, Noë, Slider, Bearmeouts, Cyclops, Tremor, Hushlushes, Nishgut, Nasaltwang, Mme Practice, Otototot, Hemdlachs, Taignit, Presha, Blume, Eichel—the many who sipped Ada's punch after music in Garden.

Little was playing—shod in one place, unswayed outstripping flights of fingering all true pitched to the bow arm —Dala saw its sinuous excellence, but heard nothing. His heart hurt, his lungs forbidden a gasp. He felt breath on his nape, and turned partly to face a furious puffing from Betur's cigarette. In the little space there was he extended his left palm forward, somewhat above his knee, with the most thoughtful gesture of inviting Betur to squeeze in front of him where politeness felt Little's teacher should stand. But Betur lighting a chain cigarette and shaking his head from side to side held Dala where he was, for an instant with the pressure of a hand on his shoulder, as tho to hide behind him, with a thankful look at Dala for shielding him. Far-sighted, intently listening, Betur obviously wanted no one behind him in his corner.

If Dala had turned deaf by a freak of mind (or *lusus naturae* as some still say) while his son was playing, the applause he now heard was deafening. "Could you hear him?" he pleaded to Betur, "Esor's bass, too, sounded very faint." The reproach which faced him was more than he had hoped for: a contorted handsome face whimpering, averting the tears, "He was won'r'ful!" And Betur stalked off recomposed thru the crowd to shield the pupil of his eyes from the visitors "countenanced" by Garden's rule only on Saturdays. His hawk vision had seen one dentist collector of fiddles speaking to Little, very likely minimizing the tone of his instrument, which was only a half-size; perhaps putting vain thoughts in the boy's mind, telling him the Guarneri, the Stradivari never bothered to make them.

"You bet you were won'r'ful and *he* knows it"—meaning Betur: Verchadet flared at her men, impatiently turning the key to the Castle, "But where was Warlock!" Her question had occurred to them quietly. "What's the matter?" Balo swallowed. "What's the matter?" Little said. "In the hoo-hah of it, all those false best wishes," she almost wept —she had been approached by Mrs Bearmeout, who had it "in confidence": Warlock had been in Garden that day, but only to look at Tremor's purchase of a Stradivarius and to talk over with Betur the young Cyclops' debut under the impresario's management at Great Hall in the fall of next year. " 'And now Eichel was worried'—as if I cared!"

"Chatterminestra," Little said not looking up from *Aga-memnon* to Verchadet, "am I to suffer another version of this *tradegy?*" He was ten, and trying to read a not too happy translation of the Greek. "And what has Mahmud," Verchadet pronounced it Ma Mud, referring to herself as much as to Betur, "*done* to deserve your faith?" "I put no faith in him and don't mistrust him *yet,*" Little said. She recalled Tearilee's name for Dala (an aside) when she first met him—*The Turk,* elicited by Dala's gentle insistence on some trifle he'd rather avoid as *he* saw it. Uncompromised future compromiser of battles Dala did not look up from obstinately, silently sounding Aneirin:

> Gear a grief's ascent be ant geat night
> girt eye gilled o wade we eye hay night
> agh y' be at anger is good dour angry man
> agh yet heel descend weal a dash sand
> nev 'r eye teem here neat at coursin'

"When has my advice been wrong," Verchadet per-sisted, "all I said was what Mihcaoj who played Bach for violin alone said before me—the prodigy grows up and the child remains. You're too good a player to beat the second-raters to Great Hall. Last year you were quick to see thru the business, older you swallow its insults. Why?" "Be-cause in business insults are not false, they're evident,"

Little parried. "O you're *so* witty beside the point," she said out of patience, "if I were variously gifted, like you, I'd know I've had enough lessons, and do something else now to support my fiddle later, if that's what you must do. *And* I'd tell Betur to keep his scholarship *and* Theory III for his other children until the year they qualify for Theory I. By that time Betur might show more interest—in you." "I'm not so sure you don't want your child to remain and a prodigy to grow up," Little said, "besides my scholarship doesn't cost us anything, and education should never be expensive." "There you hurt us both," Dala said, "that's hardly *our* consideration. The obligations that go with accepting a scholarship can turn out to be costly for the unowned artist—and money, sometimes the little that's there, money—" "So?" Little queried, expecting more logic. "Cannot—to us," Dala said.

Wintering in the brownstone, Verchadet—as Little turned a cliché—"to give me the doubt of her benefit"— declined to take the subway with him to lessons and theory. Dala asked to go with him: Little had once nearly lost a shoe, when the vise of a train's shutting doors closed on the family together but slipped his shoe off him for a kind lady on the platform to return it at the next stop. So it was on one of these self-effacing journeys (when Little would have preferred Dala to stay home) it happened while Little was packing his fiddle out of earshot and patting the boxers: Betur, aware Verchadet had not been accompanying Little to the lessons and perhaps fearing she was not at the piano during his practice at home, commended Little to Dala, "He plays very well, you know—please remember me to Mrs von Chulnt." Dala thanked him and, since Betur had confided that much as it were, added: "Little told us the summer before last that you said Mr Warlock would hear him at his debut in Garden this past summer, and we've wondered what prevented him." Betur, first as tho he hadn't heard, said after a longish pause: "Little must have misun'stood, I am sure it was a misunderstanding. I cannot tell Mr Endor what to do, I can *if he asks* sometime only speak as teacher of pupil, I am an honest man." A more negative conviction followed abstractly: "I am not sure early appearance in Great Hall helps anybody, it is better to study and hold on to merchandise for later."

Dala kept no secret from Little or Verchadet, and Little conveyed the "soap-stance of Betur's position," as hissing it he told her at once on coming home. "How did you guess he did not speak sooth, you—" he dramatized after Dala's old friend R. Z. Draykup—"you always guess right." Relenting to his show of ebullience she said, "You get one more chance, I take it you want Ma Mud to go to the mountain" —meaning Endor as Little (Baron) was quick to gather. "That makes sense," said Dala. "As *ho oikeús* of this house," she said to him, feeling the Greek word appropriate, "*you* can phone Warlock's secretary."

"Miss Shield, Mr Endor's secretary," her voice remembered Dala and offered to "connect" him with the impresario, "if he's in." "Why, yes, I've wondered what happened to Little—you say you went to Betur?" Warlock questioned affably. Dala for once listened and heard him say, "Yes, I shall be glad to hear how he's grown. Come directly this time to my little hall with the flat ceiling. Its acoustics are not so good if one sits in the middle of it. But that's where I've auditioned the best of them—all my concert artists. I shall have time for several accompanied pieces and one unaccompanied." The von Chulnts paid Flutit for some hours of rehearsals, assuring Little "more than less" of the pianist's compliance, and the four greeted Endor together.

Warlock had two undeclared reasons for sitting in the middle of his little hall: 1) if Little's half-size could be heard there, it would be heard anywhere in Great Hall, where the acoustics, contrary to the fears of the unaccomplished, actually aided accomplished virtuosity, 2) the impresario wished to be affected by the "projection" (as is said in the trade) of the performance rather than the close impassivity of the performer, which had impressed him sufficiently the first time he heard Little play. On his part Little, aware that the music would carry best to the dead spot under the flat ceiling if he enforced Flutit's compliance to accuracy, took extreme care not to project his fingerboard toward Warlock. So while the music moved impeccably for his ear, Endor put off by Little's wrapped up stance and profile found himself looking mostly at one hip and the slightest convex below it of the player—feeling it an insult absolutely intended. The audition over, "My— you've matured, very fine," he said—"why didn't you face me?"

Little felt let down inside him, but his face showed nothing to conciliate Endor. "You'll need a better fiddle, this half-size may not carry safely in Great Hall," the impresario said. "Relsierk said," Dala half queried, "that except for the ease a fine fiddle offers the virtuoso, audiences can't tell the rare instrument apart from the inexpensive." "Ah, yes, he's said it," Warlock replied knowledgeably, "but has publicized his three Guarneri." No one explicitly mentioned a debut in Great Hall. "Well, keep up with Betur," Warlock said, "and come back again, speak to my secretary on your way out to arrange it."

"Mr Endor will be away most of the spring and fall," Miss Shield explained, "you may meanwhile arrange for a city recital with our affiliate Metro Management, if you are disposed to cover the necessary box office receipts in advance." "But Mr Endor will cover those for Tremor Cyclops next fall," Verchadet came out with it, "and isn't Little just as worthy?" "Mr Endor doesn't cover anybody," Miss Shield said, "even Ztephiah Achsai must assure Mr Endor that the attendance will pay for Great Hall. And young Mr Cyclops, who's older by the way than Little, has proved immensely popular in Curaçao."

28

"Since you cannot escape inviting Betur to Great Hall, Little, you should tell him about our signed contract with Metro Management," Verchadet argued against obstinacy several months later. "He promised and says he didn't," Little gritted his teeth. "I'm in no hurry to invite him, it's not even May and my concert is in Octember, and I'm not going to Garden for him to *prepare me* (quote) with *his* stale program—if *I* feel like it *I'll* concede later to one transposed concerto for Flutit's flushing piano, or compliment them both with Postlude and Fury of Einem Pferd Schmitzik for encore and that's that. My program is my affair. You be polite if you want to, don't nag me. Did you dream I'm going to Garden again to be lied to—never! Our garden's right here—the backyard—while Dala mopes in that vile Institute this summer, to keep up with the bank's equity in the old brownstone." (Actually he was quoting Verchadet.) He hesitated: "How inconsiderate of both of us can you be?" His question pitted one against the other, and he was sorry before he finished it as he sensed his punishment—her silence. He might now not get a word out of her for days. He gazed at her even more at a loss as she looked off and he remembered "as a matter of fact" (her one bit of verbiage) she had recently at her own insistence again taken over the chore of going with him to Betur's lessons, of listening to them in that den of a waiting room, where "dear Imam," she hoped, would not be likely to step in to greet her, he had been ill and was too busy teaching two makeup lessons for every one he had missed.

"You quarrel and don't think of my bursitis," Dala also dreading her silence began tentatively. "I was able to move my left arm before you started bickering." "Nevermind, don't strain it and don't tell her about it," Little said. "How many times, Little, have I asked you, since you're less likely to hurt her with silence to—" "Now *you know* I want both of you to keep still," she ordered. "Neither of you makes sense," Dala said, and then from a long distance, "when you fall out—I might as well be in the Institute where they don't know half the things I drive myself to think in my trust of them. It's all mad. We're sensible, sensible, and suddenly there is no sense." He spoke gently, without any literal intention it seemed, to his words. Annoyed as both were with him, they could not help feeling the something of a classic frenzy that probably frightened people as often he made sense. "We've been practical for once," he said, "let's not spoil it. This concert should be as it happens, with no regrets that it might have been arranged —with other's luck—by Warlock. I rather trust Miss Shield and believe the art of bōwing is evidently for those who pay management, even Ztephiah pays before he plays," he looked at them vaguely. "If you find it so noble," Little taunted him, "you play my concert and wait until you're forty odd to mature for Great Hall. By the way when's your birthday, Lada?" "You're so sure Betur lied," Dala said sadly, "and we don't really know he did, do we? may never know. Or whether he can recommend or can't, or what his influence, or if he has any, or if after some Oriental system he looks on would be sons in size place and favors the oldest first tho he likes them all." "He's downright upwrong, if he likes us all," Little said. "But it does seem common sense even if we can't prove it," Dala said, "that a reputable teacher like Betur would not run Endor's business to be exposed in a conflict of interests?" "If you're so generous and aseptical, Sir Horse, you verify, here's the telephone, you tell him about your contract with Metro Management, I'm only Betur's baby," Little said. Verchadet's face lightened with the slightest smile. Dala was strangely aware that Little had been perusing the dictionary. It was of course the star shower of Little's puns and affection that bursitis could not twinge that fired Dala to the telephone—and his fate. He explained.

"I say iss no gut," he heard, "why you want?" Was this the suave Betur, or by some quirk his assistant Vasily Presha, Dala apprehended psychically. "We don't—or we do only because Little wants this recital," Dala said. "No! impossible, Little und'stand, you don't. Little is my friend —*you* want, I say cancel," Dala heard with Verchadet and Little straining to listen to either side of him. "I hope he will always be your friend, that's what a good teacher earns as I know it after a pupil goes on on his own," Dala said as to a friend. The voice in the receiver sounded exactly what it meant to say: "You're not my friend, Little is, you follow your teaching, I know what I know. I expect you will cancel the contract." Dala, disgusted with having said too much, blurted: "You make no sense, I can't cancel what I've signed to." "Then I won't teach," Betur said loud enough for Little and Verchadet to hear. "Don't teach," she spoke right into the mouthpiece now out of Dala's reach, and, as she hung up slowly, the receiver rattled, "b . . but Miz von Chulnt we must talk."

29

"And what will you play?" Verchadet asked. "Friends again," affectionately offering to rap her head with a restraining downward flapping of his vibrato hand, "My own program for the innocent progress of Betur, tho the reviewers may say he prepared me," Little said. "Perilex," he flashed, cabalistical, "danger—Dala—Phaethon Weaver's *5 Pieces—5 Stars—5 notes ascending the lantern crowning the cupola,* tho our pseudo friends will not like it sha'n't I be original?"—as Dala half heard over Hywel and Aneirin and wondered what Little meant, but did not dare being asked, "Where have you been living?" His son's choice predated by some years the octogenarian composer I. Gloss Dazzling's acknowledgment of his debt to the genius of Phaethon, who were he alive would always be one year younger than Dazzling.

The telephone rang. "I've a hunch it's the mountain again calling on Mahmud," Verchadet said, "I'll take it upstairs." Betur had called back almost at once after *their disconnect,* as he abbreviated perhaps after talking with Ada, to concede to Little's recital, if the contract date could be delayed *only one manth.* He would speak to Warlock about it to save the Professor embarrassment. ("Good, that leaves me out of it," Dala then noted, tho she had taken care to tell Betur she would pass on the message and that incidentally since Mr von Chulnt would have to be elsewhere the coming summer the family would not be coming to Garden. "Not necessary," Betur said. "I have confidence Little practice me because he wants. There will be time for rehearsal and dress rehearsal if we have until November. He's fast, as you know, and it's better always to play freshly.") "Tell him," Little called after her as she climbed, "that this isn't like his old joke of his school friend who didn't want to play his exam, pleading a *colt* that would spoil the varnish of the fiddle—tell him I'm not competing with who'ver he wants to play in October, I'll only be more original a month later!" "You tell him," Verchadet said, "I shall only list your program so he will feel he arranged it." Little's eyes teared perhaps for an instant grateful for her support. "Squall," Dala said with tact, looking at him thru his bifocals.

30

Verchadet and Little worked in the garden on the upper level of their city back yard. Dala wrote in the shadow of the privet, his eggshell (he called it) protected, under his Borsalino, from neuralgia the sun's direct rays always caused at a small table on the uneven pavement of the damp terrace below. She clipped a blossoming spray of privet hanging over the neighbor's wire fence, but kept it arching for shade and for them. "Much too much sun for the morning glories," Little said. Their large leaves had become a weed as he untangled a small brier from them to train it on the rock back wall. "Mostly thorns," he said. Then, overseer, he walked toward the hydrangea. "Hope springs coternal," he officiated, some eight feet above Dala, blending his Latin and Greek—*eternal* and *cothurnal*. "It's a far growth from the stump it was in Admir's sandbox when her governess, no less, wondered why it didn't grow. Cockeyed little cherub she could look mature with her blue-rimmed eyeglasses, painting the radiators with vegetable colors at three—you remember the mess we moved in on, when we exchanged apartments. She forgot to say good-bye to me and I missed her left to myself in our brownstone when she moved to the country: inconsiderate of her after all the lunches she invited me to and the rhymes we made up together to the weathervane of the retired fireboat in the dock where the old firemen held out." "That's what I call remembering," Dala heard Verchadet say, "you weren't much older, are you sure you're not repeating what I told you." "Obviously you can't remember for me more than Betur could," Little said, "Let me talk with this philosopher," and abruptly ran down the steps to the terrace to distract Dala with a slight snort: "Philosopher, your company."

Little with both hands on the top slat of the chair pushed most of his weight on him. "Ah, Manawyddan, son of Llyr," Dala said, "still a trace of your summer cold? I'm inclined to say this is finished, would you read it to me, please?" he asked removing his glasses. *"Parens., Hywel ab Owain Gwynedd—*

> panic air eke it pan arc y'pate frying
> a league grew three   fate
> a' quietly argued
> a gat land a granary gruelled"

"Does it make sense?" Dala said shyly. "Maybe—the noises, but they won't translate back into Welsh. You always seem to be wanting to say something else—like Mrs Bearemout's letter we received yesterday, about all the excitement in Garden because I'm preparing my recital myself, Betur perhaps put her up to—" "Then it does," Dala said. Little then read the last line in Dala's notebook: *"Parens., Aneirin*

> lour mom ai dagger are y' ham rant

You may have noticed," Little said, "it's some time I've dropped my middle name Baron from my autograph, it takes too long signing."

Little's cold went with the summer, and Dala's head avoided neuralgia from the hot sun. Three months without his complaints the other two were grateful. Soon like a music box taken down from an upper shelf the musical year ground its round again—October—Verchadet bringing in bouquets of crisp globes of hydrangeas for a winter's display.

31

in sanie

semper

mon chair Dala

I am Dee-lighted that you-ah *coq de combat*
has spurred a recital in Megalosaur, and foresee
in ten years a series of such (recitals) as his range
browdens. From what I hear'd here of his J. Batch
it should bring him glory, if less e-mid-jet bliss to
his progenitor. BUT all need NOT be LOSS e'en
while you "hold" the unstringed purse. A sentiment of old daze of bein' regisseur calls me
a-gayne. I can get no reprieve to come myself, and
know yew feel as I do that for every Luna tick
within these walls there are millions tick out there.
IF you can get some of 'em to ATTEND. I mean
—if you can PAPER Great Hall. 'N'if yew see no
objection I shall be glad to contack my list here
of such as still whirl in the world. Better not send
me tickets, nor (xcep very few) direct, as they
WILL lose or forget them. Let me exact promises
and send you list of those *pledged* to honor rite to
a seat picked up the night of the concert—*at the
box office.* Overheard Self-announcements would
add mystery of distinction to Little's audience.
Cannot hurt if Baroness Yolda occupies a box (she
needs) and / or two with her circle, or if Princess

Lwan Tan officiates in tiara in another with Unique
& other chawmed males.
    Fair once use yer horse topknot and doan shy.

                    Yrs

                    RZ Draykup

Durable fire singing an old tune filled Dala's mind: the
sane mad RZ *from itself never turning,* heartened and
heartening in *that* madhouse cold. "Sith the practice of the
world is to be impractical," as R once summed it up talking, Dala wrote at once to thank him for bothering—pretending to look off (with glazed eyes) when Little said, "*He
is a friend.*" "Tho how else but PAPER," Dala's afterthought followed. "Charge a friend for what I have paid?"
"Feign *free* with the throng."

Over a plan of Great Hall's orchestra, loges, dress
circle, first and second balconies, and four tiers of boxes—
the claws as it were of ascending horseshoes, in the revers-
ing order of a climbing heart's unprivileged status Verchadet and Dala PAPERED. And grieved: if with absolute
equity they could give everyone the best seat. The first Law
would not let them. Yet they tried. 2,999 seats, Ztephiah
and Neitsnebur alone were known to fill them by advance
sales months before their concerts. Of the late overflow allowed in on *their* concert nights the fire laws permitted as
many standees as ticket speculators contriving with ushers
could crowd away from the exits; also several rows of spec-
tators, weaker for their money, pitted on folding chairs on
the stage where they became part of the distraction of the
properly seated audience—especially when the aloof di-
minutive Ztephiah and no taller but lively Neitsnebur
stepped out for curtain calls, the violinist from behind his
accompanist's keyboard, the unseen harpsichordist from
behind his, and when they remembered bŏwed to the folding chairs, swallow tails arched over the footlights instead
of unobtrusively away from these for the greater plaudits.
But in the case of so young an artist's debut Metro Manage-

ment finally told the von Chulnts there were no such problems. A maximum of 299 tickets left at the box office two weeks before the concert would be more than enough to meet the demand for cash sales they might hope for. Of course that left 2,700 tickets to do as they wished with.

"There must be ten easier ways," Verchadet said summarizing for Dala the trials, comforts and errors of 800 telephone calls pursued further by correspondence enclosing tickets expected to cross their lives again—Little's sustaining audience in Great Hall—as follows:

> *Orchestra.* Rows A-B: critics (pro-Metro), last minute purchasers (sustaining?) box office (also scattered seats for them thruout Hall). Rows C-N: Dala's colleagues, faculty, wives, their friends, batches for Dr Conrad Cubinis' Shellac Bureau Importers Associates, Chairman Rumples' Apogamicfungi Society, Dean Kittenhoare's Civic Club. Rows O-Z: family, city and select country friends, neighbors.

> *8 Loges.* 4 tickets max. each: (2 center) Yolda, Tiara (recognizable distinguished authors now dispersed thru Rows C-N Orchestra, following Draykup's latest advice); (3 Right) Imam & Ada, two violin virtuosi in separate loge (Betur's request), Warlock & Associates; (3 Left) President & Mrs Gluck Coma with 2 Distinguished Trustees, President & Dean (Betur's Institute), Little's theory teacher by herself.

> *Dress Circle.* Sweetsider and Garden contingents, Presha, Blume &; Metro office staff, night help etc.

> *First Balcony.* Students, families, Dala's and Betur's Institutes.

> *Second Balcony.* Students other music schools (nominal fee passes, unreserved seats valid concert night).

Boxes. Orchestra Level. (L) Dr Gluillens; (R) Misses John Alden, James Madison, Messrs Viertel Achtel, Gwyn Yare. *Dress Circle Level.* (L) Dea Falin; (R) Misses Nasaltwang, Nishgut. *First Balcony Level.* (L) Curt Budder family; (R) Jon the marine's party. *Second Balcony (L & R).* For children who like to climb & hang over?

Estimated total 2,693, leaving two Orchestra tickets, Row E on outside aisle near the stage entrance—for Little's scrap book and for our own use during the concert in case he doesn't want us backstage during encores; the other five for emergency should Esfelts, Hiram, or the young Count forget Tearilee's or Murda-Wonda's tickets (five each to remind them) as an excuse for seeking us backstage before the concert.

[As happened.] "Why do you anticipate?" Little fretted, "I'd rather they'd listen than whisper comfortably when I play. No one will thank you for the best seat when their eyes chance on the next one. When you pay to PAPER the Hall it isn't easy for the complimented NOT to envy the music. I could do as well with one-third *that* audience." Dala sensed something sensible in Little's gripe, but tired said listlessly: "I found it hardest to remember that the odd seats in the orchestra 101, 103, 105 etc are on one side of the center aisle, and 102, 104, 106 on the other. I hope I did not send ordinal numbers to those I want to sit together." In one instance at least he was lucky, tho no omniscient observer was the wiser for it: thinking of 100 and 101 consecutively he sent 102 and 104 to his friends the poets Narodnev and Hecsteud who would be surprised and delighted to meet again after twenty years living around the corner from each other. Had he placed them in ordinal numbered seats each would have faced a malign disguise who would at once recognize him as Narodnev or Hecsteud.

32

"Going on twelve," Little said after puffing on twelve candles celebrating his eleventh birthday. "Everyone has so much to do about my Great Hall debut," he teased Verchadet—"nervous?" "Purchases," she said. He needed the largest size *boy's* formal shoes—the widest for standing thru his concert in comfort. "Not easy to come by, they might have to be ordered, along with a tuxedo?" she questioned. "I guess so," he replied not the least prest, "Nihunem's days of velveteen shorts and bare knees are gone, let Betur's *registered* or Serp's nobles wear what they will, I won't be there for ruches." She remembered how he had once sent his toy Navy blue, American red and white leather dog with Admir instead of himself to school. "Well, you had better go with Dala on one of his free days soon and at least see what you can find ready made," she said without seeming to urge him.

In the five weeks before the evening of Little's first recital in Great Hall, the trio found time to buy his concert wardrobe. Verchadet, whom Little persuaded to come along, again suffered the beginning of a tale Dala's honesty would in time relive to his own discredit. He had led them straight to a legendary turn of the century department store and genteel shoes. Bemused by his success, eyes lowered toward the floor but following the tied shoe box under

Little's arm, he nearly missed seeing the satin trim on two stylish legs of midnight blue cloth: the color almost indistinguishable from black that never browns or grays. "Sir, where are the tuxedos?" he asked without looking up. When Little and Verchadet tittered Dala raised his head to catch himself addressing a mannequin. "Laud nose: knows," Little scored. "Doesn't a nose lead," Dala said, "now if only they have your size." What blessed idiot spoke of *mental music?* The mulled note sounded: *Eskimo fashion a man and a little boy once rubbed noses*—'Nose-ick.' The store *had* the size requiring *no* alteration. Dala was content having shopped as he had planned. Had he tho? His taste wavered once his purchases were made. Did quotations pursuing themselves in his head foreshow good? "No doubt they rose. .Valentine. .wood-birds. .can no longer live by thinking"—the quotations decided. "Don't forget my tuxedo," Little said, "some day you and I will write an opera and you may need a tuxedo." "I won't forget your tuxedo and don't you forget the opera," Dala smiled, for no reason vaguely visualizing the Great Wall of China he hadn't in some years. "By the by," Little said, "while they were packing the tuxedo I read an item about Ztephiah Achsai making his debut and *for years* his career on an indifferent, what did they call it, *biscuit tortoni* or something, even *now* not worth more than two grand—how much is it, Verch?" Little was of course hoping for a contingency.

In the five weeks before the evening of Little's debut in Great Hall, Betur suffered the fears which his pupil's summer's absence from Garden obliged him to dispel as *the stretch*. The first words Betur said to Little on their reunion were, "Half-size won't carry." He ran from his studio and returned shortly to display the unwrapped three-quarter violin in its battered case. With a tenderness reserved for a newborn infant, "I borrowed for *you*," he said. It might have been his. "You see with like boy's treble stretch change." "I know," Little said as the wise might after having simply observed. But with the three-quarter under his hands and fingers shifts and intervals soon leaped accurately. "Not too moch the first time," Imam cautioned, "might hurt 'self stretching." "Don't worry," Little said. "I say *worry,*" Betur recalled a previous summer, then added slowly, "See, if you strain would hurt concert. Enough today."

The sliding doors opened an inch to Ada whispering, "Mme Otototot has just stopped by." "Must?" he said. "I am afraid so," she said and told him what Verchadet had despite herself overheard behind the drawn portieres of the waiting room. The sobs and tears of Mme Otototot could not dampen the news that the older Hemdlach sister had passed away after willing her grand piano to Garden. Her last breath had *ordered* it be delivered at once. "Now?" he asked. "A strange bequest," Ada said, "but where shall I store it meanwhile with our three pianos here?" "In the studio," he said in fidelity to the deceased, "until I can arrange with the long distance movers." Verchadet again overheard the voice which could not whisper, brighter from the end of the hall: "Imam, how's my boy doing?" Thinking of Little but speaking to Ada Betur said, "He has a head not just to hold a fiddle up." Little was too absorbed packing the three-quarter size into his own case to hear. *"Un moment,"* Betur waved backward to Mme Otototot while Little caught up with him at the portiere he held back to greet Verchadet, their dispute of last spring conveniently forgotten. "Miz von Chulnt," he asked earnestly after suggesting three free lessons a week during the remaining weeks before the recital, "please see he does not overdo." "I don't control Little. But *you* must not overdo, Mr Betur. Two lessons would be more than a great kindness," she said uncompromised. "Then two," he agreed as tho she had, "beginning next week. Would happen I moss go to Garden out of season," he added to his pupil's bewilderment. In

Little's mind his fingers had been on *the stretch* effecting the higher positions—why this a—*non squitter* (he punned to himself on his Latin) to Garden? Compassing *the stretch* was as painless as growing up in tuxedo trousers on every upbow the evening of his debut in Great Hall. Lucy Drischay, her listening limited to watching their rhythmical lift, told Verchadet that they were two inches short—mentioning it only with the future of *her* nephew in mind. And so many hellos out of the hollows of Great Hall, generous and envious saying the playing was beautiful, asked why didn't he smile. The leading newspaper critic in his lead column echoed: "A child with *nary a* smile, but a program that might give older virtuosity pause —in short, stretch of his fingers on the button and a bow arm of threatening genius to match."

Two dress rehearsals with Betur standing in front of every acoustically critical seat in empty Great Hall had calmed his fears that "an important pianissimo" might not be heard the night of Little's recital. "It will be heard more properly," he assured Little, "with full audience as soundboard." It was during this second rehearsal that Verchadet, by chance turning her head, saw Warlock slink in and out at the rear of the dark orchestra. She soon forgot him, settled comfortably with Dala among the vacant rows of seats —both callous to Imam's remote consultations with the soloist and his accompanist onstage. For the parents the two rehearsals replaced the debut with the added delight of a repeat performance. For guarding the wings from friends on the night of the concert they would be listening backstage, handing out and taking back the music so the players could proceed smoothly between bŏws. Verchadet and Dala both took it for granted the debut would excel the rehearsals. But Dala huddled with fever on the night of the recital could not convince her or Little that it was *not* the recital which distressed him.

From Little's first note on she was happy there was no

one to talk to, singing—a faint hum in her throat—the violin part Little had left with her—Dala on his folding chair hushing her under his breath as he tried to listen shivering in his overcoat. Her humming did not stop, and he could not sit. He rose to a temperature of 103 and walked to the coulisse to steady himself with a glimpse of Little's bow arm, but she motioned him back to his folding chair—not for long. He rose again to peer thru a chink in the backdrop, for all his aches a stagehand overseeing all's well. But unable to see anything of Little, his eyes focused on someone he had known and could not name in a seat he had 'papered.' She let him be, knowing he would sit down and be up again, while she gave Flutit the piano score of the concerto Betur had picked for the showpiece before intermission. She appeared almost too happy to Dala when Little's razzle-dazzle tidily eased Flutit over an accompanist's blunder. And in the second half of the program, as Dala deplored biblically in his fever, her felicities seemed to outweigh the years before Jubilee: gay, gay with the Bach solo partita, with the Weaver Imam had refused to teach leaving complete responsibility for it to Little, with the Mozart Allegro for balance. Betur was the first, after tipping a cordon of ushers, to congratulate Little in the green room. Verchadet, who had hurried ahead to avoid the immediate deluge of cranks and autograph seekers, foreboded from Betur's crisp judgment how the reviewer would read next morning: "Good, but smile sometime gives audience confidence. *Bot* good. Glad you played on'y two encores, not like who was—coming out to ask, 'you want anodder?' Don't get tired now you know what 's all about. Moss go—getting late —we speak at lesson."

"Remember my old neighbor Bach? Ah Snorckie what a concert!" For an instant Little hesitated over the sound of his childish name he had not for some time been called by. "Ah yes!" Little greeted, "Count Murda-Wonda?"—who had left his bed "to make it . . . such impeccable, unsentimental Mozart . . . Who was that gentleman? I heard what he said about smiling, and I see no reason why you should have to the pigs I sat next to!" The Countess, young Count and the others stood by abashed, so that Little made the mistake of not recognizing them. "Lucy" Esfelt (of course Little had the name wrong) said, "The Sabbath— almost any day of the week now—prevented grandma Tearilee from coming, but you know she *really can't* bear the strain of watching you play."

Aging friends from Sweetsider, Garden, where—shook Little's hand and left. A wizened, obviously musical lady in figured lilac organdy, at last approached Dala whose fever had subsided into the demands on his courtesy. "Dea Falin," she said, "Sweetsider Church. You are so kind to have thought of me. Your son was even more wonderful today. Please congratulate him and yourselves—no, I must not impose." The electrician was dimming the lights, and telling everybody to leave. "I will," Dala swallowed, insisting on leading her carefully from the green room and downstairs to the exit. "I looked for old Warlock in his usual loge," she said vaguely, "in all his evil years he has refused to meet me. He wasn't there tonight, only his disaffected associate I would never speak to. Thank you, I live nearby." By this time Little and Verchadet catching up behind them had heard what she had said about Warlock. They nodded to her as Dala held the door for her, and again before they turned the street corner for the subway home.

When leaning over one another they read the review the next morning Little paled somewhat and said nothing. Dala, who read the last sentence (the reader has read before) first, flared to the sting of the adjective "threatening" before "genius." As he read backwards he was even more infuriated by the reviewer's guileful attentions to Flutit and Betur as Little's teachers. The ring of the telephone interrupted the cheerless von Chulnts and Little went to answer it. Verchadet and Dala were so still most of the impulse coming from the receiver reached them. "Little? Betur. The reviewer," he said, "know nothing. When 's good they say *bad*, and when 's bad they use word like *'strawdinary* or *unb'lievable*. Pay no attention—we speak at lesson." "Thanks," Little hung up without turning to his parents who had more or less overheard. "I guess your friend had nothing to say about "mangement," Verchadet said brooding on Dea and Warlock. "No calls from impresarios— only a lesson on Monday 8 A.M." "I'm not listening," Little said, hurrying up three steps at a time to his room. Dala felt *nothing* inconsolably inside him. "It's easy for Imam to say 'they come, *mangement* come,'" she said— "I'm tired, I'd rather not remember." "Don't," Dala said. "Well, if he wants to he can be insulted again," Verchadet said meaning Little.

He reappeared for lunch two hours later. "Medusa Flutit," he started out, expecting his pun involving upper and lower case would make them happy, *"would* make the same mistake at the recital that Betur called him down for at the second rehearsal. 'Jellyfish,'" he glossed when neither smiled. "I forgot to tell you," he persisted, "because giving up my *dairy*" (here both eyes winked) "is no aid to the memory: the other day Jellyfish complained of a backache from sitting down so long and having to repeat his run three times to get it right. Betur said: 'Pliz, listen, don't wash! It won't matter if you play the recital half sitting down, half standing up. *Bot* keep time reg'lar. Strongk! like washwoman in Bretagne river! Where—how—you going—Luxembourg, Istanbul, Vienna, Warshawa, Bucharest, Reykjavik, Curaçao?'"

33

"Fugue or phugh, almost spring term, and I'm tired of abiding immortal Theory III on *Sat'days*," Little yawned slightly to Verchadet in January after his Great Hall debut by then safely historical. "I told Betur this morning—" For two months he had been riding the subway by himself to continued violin lessons on Mondays. "I told him," he finished his yawn, "that I have my high school diploma and I am ready for college." "And did you ask him why the advanced student should be retarded," Verchadet said. "Shut—" Little said too briskly, "but excuse me, Betur is not my enemy!" "Nor your friend," she said as tho unconcerned. "If you'll listen—" Little began again: "First, he missed his chance to sing at the opera, he has a *colt*—but he's not sorry about that; worse he has to save himself for 'worse engagement' tomorrow when the Musical Institute of Neufafen 'extinguishes' him with an honorary doctorate, 'I need a doctor's like waste time,' he sighed," Little laughed looking toward Verchadet. She looked the other way. " 'But why violinist need college to take time from practice,' " Little quoted Betur, " 'we renew your Institute scholarship and maybe arrange special Theory IV on Fridays when you would be the *only* pupil. I know Administration consider you too yong for Institute Upper School, bot *why* you need *humonities* course? I' sure you learned already.' " "Constant and neutral, along with of course free lessons," Verchadet said, looking noble with her least smile. "I see I can't get advice from you," Little chided.

He could always interrupt Dala in the little room opposite the largest in the brownstone. Dala disliked spreading thru space, preferred things small and compact, a small table for desk, a narrow shelf of books over it: so that when he was not writing it was a blank table, never a display of creativity or a sign such as exhorted him in a colleague's study, THINK. But this time when Little breezed in Dala was ghosting—for a banker—between ever heavier chores for his Institute at his permanently stalled salary. An oversolicitous friend, who had ghosted the banker's previous books—of a political campaign nature against government that assumes too much—had tendered Dala this extra income. And when his friend assured Dala and the banker face to face that Dala would do better by the banker's latest than 'I myself have time to do,' Dala and the banker both appeared gratified by their bit of luck. Dala, as he told Little, had been unreserved with the banker, *told him* that while von C might not agree with B's ideas—obviously a banker could not satisfy everybody—that B must tell von C, whenever in doubt, what B wanted to say—that as a writer von C must be sure he is the banker's true statement and ghost. As it turned out (the book's faithful eloquence delighted the banker so, he could never find a publisher for it) Dala's great difficulty was as Verchadet said, some ideas are just not clear: and she stood often over his editing to see that a word from the point of view of hourly pay did not bankrupt him for an age. So when Little breezed in Dala's small table *was* cluttered, tho in seeming orderly fashion, to his distaste, with the banker's original elegant typescript, three pages of handwritten editing in sequence, a neat pile of ninety-nine blue examination books to be corrected for his Institute classes, and last year's Institute Catalog he had been assigned to revise "minimally" for this year. Little always had the right to pick up anything from Dala's small table, tho Dala had no right to displace anything on Little's large desk in his room, and Little picked up the Catalog. "What is this *Strength of Materials* course," he asked Dala, "like *Materials of Music*, Theory III?" "I guess so, but for engineers, not music students," Dala answered not looking up. "What was the question?" he asked some minutes later, "O I remember, why do you ask?" "Would *Strength of Materials* be more *viable* than *Materials of Music*, Theory IV—I know music takes in its physics, and physics does not go out of its way for music, or will it? But if as Manawyddan said, if need be sometime we have to do our work elsewhere—" Little stopped talking, looked at Dala's face, then away a distance as tho he were travelling the railroad with his fiddle. "What can I say," Dala said, "knowing little of either, merely human enough to believe that both physics and music are humane." "Probably neither is humane," Little said. "Does your Engineering Institute grant scholarships for the same sham humane reason as mine, which flatters a minor into thinking it costs nothing to be a violin major forever?" "I suppose physics might be as easy for somebody as music, I didn't know you were thinking of changing—" here Dala stopped, then added: "Would you want me to ask my President about a scholarship for you? The Institute has some fringe benefit offering free tuition to sons of professors with tenure and little means. When he called me in to discuss the new curriculum the other day he greeted me by your first name, assuming it's mine. He was enthusiastic about your debut, which he attended you know—said he *envies* you, still dreams of conducting an orchestra, having himself majored in *sound*." "This convinces me, thank you, *no*," Little said, "I'd just as soon follow mad Draykup's advice, *but you're a performer, Ewe hev to fader.*" "That's *just* it," Dala echoed slightly, "who is it's responsible, who is accountable—it happens *ewe hev to*." Here Dala lingered. "Don't be too sure about that," Little said, "you may notice I have just made my choice." "But—" but taken up by Little's new slant of thought, Dala shied at *But*, looking at Little and feeling in deed very responsible. "How can you stand it— teaching there?" Little said riled, not in the least thinking why Dala looked very responsible. "Oh—it seems all right when I'm actually there, and I vary what I must say from term to term by speaking extempore—I hope—so it doesn't mostly seem to come out of my own ears. And to new students it's new, and a few old ones say it's all they've learned. Not that what I say isn't good talk—you know I'm not proud of talking—the kind of talk maybe that gets other more serious they'd say, or shall I say less fortunate professors a Chair! But it isn't silence—well, not business either." Dala looked worried: "I hope my banker is not disappointed; that I have not falsified one word he meant to say, but if one edits can one—" "Dala," Little said to distract him from that topic, "I was trying to find it the other day, was it Parahelsus who said, 'I don't shun the music of yesterday, I look backwards new to old, not old to new.'" "No, not quite that, but very near what you just said—'You run off, I am new.'"

"For want of a Warlock, whatever your frets over Betur's intrigue with Wizard or vice versa, expect *man'ger* and find none, or as *heppens* expect none and find one." Little said on another day to Dala—apropos of nothing, as neither Dala nor Verchadet had openly rankled for some time. After nearly six years of Betur it was the teacher noticeably grown old who always seemed to run off while Little with apparent loyalty pursued him, unexpectedly from time to time with a new "chance" score of dots, dashes and carets that bypassed note, line and intensity to the discretion of the performer. About which, Betur would say, "*This* I moss leave to you, we have still Beethoven concerto to do. As for former—whether in Tabriz where I wass born, or Hamadan where I stud'ed, or Mrs Betur maybe tell you in *Jawjaw*—

would be difficult to play when's hot becus summer flies change composer's score." Betur said this with a straight face turned sadly to Gesib. The aged boxer no longer stirred to see Little off at the door. "She old lady now," Imam condoled. Her brother Sib whom both father and sister missed had suffered a brain hemorrhage, was no more. With no summers in Pamphilia and Garden, or lessons to sit thru in the waiting room stretching the time for Verchadet and Dala, soon it was eight years since Little came to Betur and played the De Bériot for him. " 'Wonderfully,' " as Guy Esor Octa, whom the von Chulnts ran into once, in his embarrassment in meeting them again, recalled Betur saying, " 'Perhaps as I shall never hear it again.' " Reminded again Verchadet was not salved on top of her recent grievance against the Administration of Betur's Institute, tho it had finally conceded to Little's matriculation in the Upper School after his solitary year of Theory IV—largely spent teaching his composer-tutor how to write for the violin. To her annoyance it was Betur who convinced the Administration to "make exception in this unusual case," after she had *submitted* (academic transcript along with annual renewal of scholarship application) and hinted how else do you expect to keep him. "But I think," Little confided to Verchadet towards the end of that year, "Betur looks forward with dread to marching with his youngest pupil in purple in June—'stupid ceremony,' he said today, and what he fears most is that I might complete my master's degree in one year. He inhaled so much smoke when I told him the Administration will let me do it, he sneezed and saluted me in German, 'Gesundheit!' He treads carefully even with his older students these days and seems resigned when he can find them a job at thirty. It isn't that he wants to teach them, but knows he has so much to teach them. Ada actually had to pin him down in his sheets and blankets when he had pneumonia yet pleaded with her to help him out of bed—he simply *had to* prepare Unzung Pharette for her recital." "She's back, then, from Istanbul?" Verchadet asked absently. "Where else would she be back from," Little answered, impatient with her, in his mind aware of Unzung's age, at least eleven years older than he—"twenty-five, if a day. She's in my Greek literature in translation class," he said, "and in her Islamic frenzy the other day asked me, 'Who is Jesus,' meaning Aegisthus. They're all that brilliant. I never answer, just mumble to myself, *Kunst der Fuge.*" "Betur doesn't give up," Verchadet scoffed. "Really, Betur's wonderful," Little differed, "true he can't demonstrate in pitch anymore, but when he plays out of tune, *'sory that wass wrongk,'* he says, as if the wrong note had been wrung from him. A little paunchy, but when he dresses up in white tie still Imam, tho he hates public occasions and is for the most part tied in by the sash of his smoking jacket." Observing Verchadet Little wasn't quite sure whether she was the least bit jealous or sad.

Meanwhile the brownstone was aging for want of repairs. The three were lucky to be out for a walk together one spring day when a large chunk of ceiling plaster rosette molding above Little's bed unexpectedly came down. Overriding his objections Dala and Verchadet *badgered* him, as he protested, into putting up with Dala's small room while they risked the larger. The next day Verchadet's left eye throbbed and reddened. "What causes it?" Dala worried. "O nothing much, the plaster dust maybe." But the following day recalling the pain a sty gave her as a little girl she took one look at the eye in the mirror and fainted—"like a classical Chinese actor in transfixed anguish, a bird settling spirally," Dala said later. He was on hand shaving, and cried out for Little as he helped her fall without hurt. He chafed her hands on the wood floor and whimpered, but Little ran and filled a glass with cold water, which he dashed into her face. "What is all this water for?" she moaned coming to, and feeling chilled she rebuffed him, "what—are you crazy?"

"Tse-tse-tse-tse," Dala chirped, for the third time in his life *having seen* (he said) *behind the Great Wall of China,* "we've had enough brownstone." Then managerially: "its basement and three stories are going up for sale, and we move to a brand new apartment where you can have less furniture all on one level. And since we won't be mortgagees sharing in equity with magnates of high finance, it's a long time we've had a vacation, we'll travel on their down payment to *us*. O di mi, on second thought," Dala spoke shyly to himself, "interest cannot be avoided on real estate transfers, but we will make the new owners happy by accepting the legal least."

When Little told Betur that the von C's had moved and were going abroad, he wished him well and impressed him "not to forget the *same* to your parents: also especially tell them it would be good you give another concert in Great Hall in February of next year. The last I think was good for you, bot if you don't come back audience forget."

Miraculously Dala's lawyer sold the brownstone faster than they expected. Verchadet, before sailing, neatly arranged their four room apartment for their return. She gave the pussy willow stems and other plants to Miss Madison who had come from the country to see them off. And before closing the door for the summer on all their possessions she secured a towel rack over the kitchen sink by *gluing* the screws into the wall lath, that is after forbidding Dala's and Little's assistance, otherwise they wouldn't have made the gangplank in time. They sailed on a small ship, an overhauled freighter—the decks crowded with students conferring, studying, lectured to, so the von Chulnts had to step over their heads or laps to get to bow or stern—seasick 9 days out of 10 in their own private cabin—to Europe.

34

"What's that he's sweeping the garden with?" Little asked. "That's a besom," Dala said. Thanks to the fine graces of Gwyn Yare, James Madison's friend, tho it would never have occurred to the von Chulnts to ask him, they had been invited to an ancient type of Betur's Garden in Cornwall. The girls and boys of Cornwall School, whose old gardener tidied a green almost blue grass, played consorts of viols. In kind Little gratified them and their master with a solo concert of bōwings and fingerings never short of Betur's method. Cornish, the children marveled and courteously served their guests three recipes of potatoes and two of tomatoes every meal of the day. The von Chulnts ate and in return praised the great stones of the medieval refectory. They stayed a week, then started their travels.

"In Rome you don't have to as the Romans and nowhere else eyether," Little said, "it sickens me when you flatter foreigners who won't speak their own language." In Oxford, a bookseller bemused by Little's fiddle case brought out a facsimile of Bach's manuscript of the partitas for him. He glanced and looked off, purchased *a tract on the oriels* instead. They then sent, *air mail*, identical souvenir postcards to their families, two to each, addressing the one of Baliol to the young, and the interior of Baliol to Murda-Wonda and Tearilee—all bearing the same greeting: *Here we are—well! Hope you are. Love.* This taken care of, they boarded the train for London without conscience, riding privately in a second class compartment. "I say," Little sounded British taunting Dala, "this arrangement disposes of your theories of *clahsses.*" "But if the national railroad were busy enough to fill the two seats occupied by your fiddle case—" Dala queried, implying in his tone—*would you feel so uppish.* Little ignored him, and now wrote on the back of his postcard of Brasenose (which Verchadet always instilling courtesy had distantly suggested he might mail from London to Betur): *Worked well in Cornwall. On to London. Kindest regards.*

In London it happened (without thinking of Great Hall ahead) they bought Little an expensive Tourte bow (*never mind the Bach one,* Little said to Dala absorbed in it, *that's vanity*) and (as they still felt the affluence of their vacation) a not at all expensive fiddle with an original belly prized for its maker—its eighteenth-century back forever broken to splinters since matched by a less esteemed early nineteenth-century violin maker, a wine merchant. "Try it," Verchadet urged, liking the yellow in its amber narrow waist. "Pretty comfortable," Little agreed as he chinned it, "but has to be played in." "Let's buy it, Little," Dala said, "since it happens this way."

They took the Channel boat and shuttle train to Paris, where on the first kiosk they saw they tried to read an old rainworn poster the print of which they could not agree about—each reading differently:

(Little)	Athé	QUATUOR
(Dala)	Ah-The	QUATUOR
(Verchadet)	ah the	QUATUOR

All agreed as to QUATUOR.

Whether in Bath or Florence, Verchadet would not condescend to the continental tour. Her test of great art was that she should not be dragged to it. It would justify itself drawing her glance, as she looked while she walked at a distance. One glimpse into the interior of a landmark was enough to keep her out. Also not sightseers Dala and Little were still afraid they might if they hurried on miss something. She waited too often impatiently for them as appearing longer for their shyness they came out from a landmark, fortifying themselves to praise a chased tendril on a tomb or the rib of a vault. Little would then *forestall the situation* "Well, Mrs Shriek—" enticing her sometimes to smile at Dala and say, "Well, Mr Weak—"

Nearly three months of travelling. After crisscrossing the Alps from Italy to Switzerland, again somehow in Italy in Switzerland and on to France, they would be recognized warmly by other travellers they *must have* met before overnight at some stop quite nameless now, tho the others knew them at once: the lean gentleman, the slight well-dressed but not showy lady, their growing son with a fiddle case, whom they greeted by his first name while the compact family longed for home. They had privately been sensing it all thru their journey in their dread of seasickness on the ship that awaited them. Again inevitably they faced the chaos of sea. Very sick indeed, the three bumbled in their cabins past the point of no return impeding and pursuing their memories at once West and East.

After the pavement of their city home stopped rolling under them, Verchadet remembered for Dala one midnight the eight wonders that had made their European vacation worthwhile:

> the besom and gaiters of the old gardener in Cornwall
>
> the porter who—having placed their luggage on the train to be delayed for two hours at Victoria Station stood by them until Dala failing to persuade him to seek elsewhere and aching for the man's loss of livelihood, having only a crown and six shillings in English money to give him asked,

"is that all right?"—shook all their hands and said, "lovely"

the French customs inspector first unduly detaining them for his tip until they understood the custom, then rushing and hurtling their luggage over ten rails, to lift each of them safely off the ground, luggage after, on to their train that had begun to pull out

from the train window near Nantes an ancient woman powerfully washing her laundry on the river stones in high tide

a publishing house still firm since the last war over the edge of a bomb crater seen at the end of a long English day

a rainstorm in Keswick on just getting off the bus from Grasmere

The North Sea come upon a bleak streak in Edinburgh—Portobello (?)—Firth of Forth—

Little's black feet, on returning to their hotel after walking several days out of the rain the whole length of the arcade called the rue de Rivoli

He had not shined his shoes once in Europe. Verchadet did not urge, resigned, he might think of doing it himself. As to *life* she felt useful people should not harass misuses. "Why are your feet so black at the end of a day?" she finally asked one evening as merely a type of question. "I don't know. I've been bathing." "Is the dye coming off your socks?" He was in the shower and did not hear her as she felt the socks thru the holes and no leather. He had worn out his concert shoes.

35

Snow was a foot high when they came out of the subway at Great Hall. Fortunately for the trousers of his first swallowtail accenting his return Little wore boots over his new concert shoes. *One cannot chase a need,* Verchadet thought herself saying. She might at this instant be thinking instead of Dala—these words not voluntarily her thought. But how extricate her legs in their boots sunk in two holes in the snow: Little way ahead hurdling pure heaps in the flaky downfall, Dala floundering behind him, not too sprightly while assuming her sense of things would lead her into the holes he sank for her in the heaps. He returned to help her trudge, making new tracks for himself.

At the stage door Little obtusely saw Betur stooping out of a taxi—in the icy flurry emptying a coat pocket of its bulge of coins to the sheltered cabby. Little did not feel like talking, but Betur caught up with him, squeezing thru to the other side of the door as it shut. "Frank," the unassuming teacher said to the guard in the drafts, "see no one disturb Mr von Chulnt till after encores, and please tell Brown to keep the crowd from the Green Room so I can hurry upstairs 'head of ev'body and go early." In asking these favors his good manners seemed to hide the exposed stance of the guard, as turning his head somewhat aside Betur thrust his customary excessive tip into the man's coat handkerchief pocket. Little's glance observed his teacher's, then his back, heavier these last few years, aching perhaps girdled under the styled tuxedo. He had heard him call him mister. Imam was—and well *was*, after eight years, *Imam*, Laila's Majnun—"Romeo" to Frank and stagehands and ushers. He was their intimate who had brought so many prodigies they could listen to for free, judge—and whose futures they weighed as said "in the balance": *young von Chulnt is great or Betur would not let him come back in two years.* In the Green Room Betur took the fiddle—anachronous belly and back—from Little's hands to examine it again and then leave him on his own. "Not bad, you know, for mongrel— and just as well: belly nicer than back." He took a last look out of habit at the bouts. If their seams had opened he could do nothing, and if he could—"it's always safest to play the fiddle one worked on." He looked around: "Careful you don't touch all this velvet furniture—they never dust here. What you might say integration make fingers slip. Good luck, see later."

Verchadet and Dala sat in about the middle of the or-chestra. This time they meant to watch and enjoy Little play. Waiting for the hall to fill they looked up into the cupola, the golden glows of the lantern above it making its white paint marble. Below—the orchestra was almost empty. They did not wish to make themselves conspicuous by craning their necks to count heads in the climbing horse-shoes. Draykup released from the madhouse and parted from them by the seas was too far to recommend again, "PAPER!" This time Little insisted, "Papering is not a fair test of an audience." His parents' thoughts ranged singly parallel. Should they have papered? Whether by papering and newspaper publicity artists find their valid audiences sooner than later? "I don't suppose many 'll appear at the other concerts tonight either," Verchadet said. She had skimmed advertisements, in Little's recital program, of sev-eral concerts elsewhere in the city that evening. "Regrets?"

"No, except why did we pick February, it's so cold," she answered him. "Still some days to wait for Valentine to give a beggar a cloak," he said indifferently himself as he touched her hand. She predicted silently their families would stay home: wasn't it true, *their* homes were their deepest wish. Not to blame them: simpler. A few rovers straggled in from the storm. Someone behind joshed about the snow stealing his stalled car. It was nearly nine o'clock when the stage lights arced and Little followed by Flutit walked out and bŏwed, both taking in how few were there. Presumably they had friends dignified only by papering. They had known these friends as not stingy with self-gratifications called "gracious." Little nodded to Flutit with a look that might say *don't coax your wares,* and played. *Not tomorrow* flitted past Verchadet's ears. *For the snow—a mysterious compliment to nature, like,* and Dala omitted the "like" in his mind—*the snow.* "Are you listening?" Verchadet urged. Dala pretending his eyelashes had misted his lenses wiped them—"Yes."

During intermission most of the small scattering of audience remained seated, advised it would be brief. The few who rose worried, two's or three's, how they would get home. Dala had got up to stretch. He saw an old man smiling, to him perhaps, shadowed by the columns supporting the loges. He was reminded of his father. Who was he? *In this storm?* he wanted to ask, but his personal remembrance, if he did, might wrong the momentary closeness he felt for a stranger. The impulse to speak passed both when someone venturesome for a glimpse of the sidewalk fronting Great Hall was hurled back by slamming doors and covered in white coils of blizzard, so that Dala without his far eyeglasses could not make out whether it was man or woman.

Soon the long concert and encores were over, Little the happiest for it—it had gone well. The night guard rushed to the stage to ask everyone to use the side exits on leaving, as the front doors were now shut. Few followed Betur to the Green Room—autograph buffs who did not lag. Betur's *good night* at the door after a hushed *good* to Little perhaps beggared intimacy when he also addressed Verchadet and Dala, "unfortunate the storm—there should've been more to hear him." Past Great Hall's alley they came out on stalled cars at all angles. Exactly when had motors refused to rev, brakes to screech, horns to stop blowing, and churned into—Dala gaped at what had been an avenue—a conclave of rear ends to bumpers, hoods to door handles, windshield wipers poised, all transmuted of the snow's hooded societies. Bent into the updraft of the subway the von Chulnts, the three together now, felt the highest tread of the entrance stairs thru snow above their boots.

The lower steps felt more certain as they tamped the snow down them. As happens in blizzards on the platform a pleasant if sparse party (they might have met these four people before somewhere?) informed them with smiles (that recognized them?) they had just missed a train. The few trains not stalled in the air were running only underground between this station and "theirs," the next in about an hour. They waited two and reached their stop at two in the morning, when after saying good night the party left them. Quietly the confetti of snow hurled down on a beaten way of friendship *Shake-spere* reminded Dala as they trudged: what responsible neighbors—asleep now (?) had cleared this path one foot wide and one foot deep for them between walls of snow taller than Verchadet? "This is great!" Little said, the gloved palm of an affectionate hand hovering above her head, as tho fearful of his son's impetus Dala cringed for her. Little's hand stopped with patting the snow of her wool hat. "This goodly frame the earth" Dala's trudging metered out for him, *the gracioso of it*—his mind flew before him as usual—*came with the effort*. It took another half hour. "A congregation of vapours," they opened their apartment house door with their own key—the night doorman nowhere around—and brushed off in the foyer.

Coats hung up and boots aligned in the bathroom, they changed into dry stockings while Dala recalled the summer evening of the hurricane when he returned from work with his shoes in his hands. "You wouldn't remember, Little"— who said (he was a year old then) "I do." To appease hunger, Verchadet faster than everybody asked Little— "and, tell me, do you want coffee?" "I have never tasted of it yet," he said. "Warm milk, then?" "Why ask? I recall tea." From their twelfth story view of the city's harbor indistinguishable from the snow they reported the blizzard to her in the kitchen. Plentiful, even courteous, as Dala now thought of it, the snow whirled its merry-go-round of profusions. "I could watch it all night," Little said. "I'd like a fire behind a fire screen," Verchadet said. "Do you really intend an all night session?" Dala asked yawning thru his nostrils. "Aren't you tired, Little? tho I wonder what the reviewers said, if there'll be any papers today—it is today."

They were gazing listlessly when the intercom startled them. "It's that smart night doorman who's back," Little said. "Mr Curt Budder," the voice announced. "Are you sure?" Dala questioned. "Saw your lights on, has two newspapers for you," and with less aplomb, "I hope I haven't— disturbed—" "No, no," Dala said, "please send him up," now aware of the name of Little's boyhood friend. "Wait, I think he's gone off," the doorman said. "Sorry, I thought he'd keep the papers for you until morning," another voice said not too near the phone, "are you sure it's all right to say hello, I can't stay." "Sure, please do," Dala persuaded him. He showed up at their door more wiry than Little, snow on matted brown hair, eyes out of an afternoon sky brilliant blue—matched against a short sailor's coat, navy corduroys, and ankle height hobnailed o-live shoes, Little punned inwardly. "Felicitations," his friend said, perhaps sounding for him a bit literary. "Come in, come in," Dala repeated. "If only to warm up," Verchadet said. "I trust that's a dry wool shirt under your elegant costume," she spoke moved by gaiety, hopefully not like a mother. "No, I like snow," he said having stopped at the threshold. "They're wet," he added for her care looking down at his shoes, "but boots in this blizzard would be wetter." He had been to the concert, he explained, and not to bother Little in the Green Room decided to walk the two subway stops to the Square and pick up the papers, since there would probably be no deliveries for days. "One review's very good, and the other—well I don't agree," he said quietly. "I expected I'd meet your train at the Square, but just missed it." "Won't you come in tho," Little asked. "No, my family came to your concert with me and must be worried where I am by now." (Were the four they met in the subway *his family*, the three thought as one—too shy to ask, never to be certain.) Little walked him back to the elevator. "We didn't urge anyone to come to this concert," he said, frankly not sorry before the one proof of his test of not papering. "Why should you have," Curt said. "It was fine, that's the difference." "Thank you," Little said, "drop by again," wondering when there'd be time. "Sure would," but he'd be with the merchant marine for a year, ultimately to get to the north woods for a while, he hurried to tell Little holding the elevator door: "I like snow, and I don't suppose this kind of weather's good for warming your fingers—see you!"

No one sifted the gist or gruel—she'd think when newspapers clogged her throat—faster than Verchadet. When Little returned from saying good-bye to Curt he saw that she had read the reviews. For Dala's ascetic back turned to the door, forehead close to window pane, eyes looking but not seeing, meant he did not want them to see his face suffering their dismay—did not want *a* thing—or if his hurt was not that serious after he excoriated it, a reserved personal note like: "the pother over birthpangs of writing, pupa sealing images at the threshold of stupefied larval thoughts—confident moths for the bonfire." "What is?" Little asked. She did not answer giving him the newspapers. "What purfles?" Little asked again, nodding toward Dala. "A friend could have done better," she said, "please, I'd like quiet." "Another seizure of Betur?" Little champed his teeth and read for himself. Of the two newspapers which fed the city's musical taste at large and—as an ample classical critic versed with an opposite slant—'not of an age,' the older less circulated paper whose senior critic's quirk or temerity was to legislate 'for all time' did not affect the violinist's *present* future. Teased by a seepage of unanimous condolement for pure mature musicality entertaining empty halls in the blizzard, Little hurried thru reviews of other concerts before absorbing his own. None of these cordial reviews mentioned competence, but in Little's case neither of his critics so much as referred to a snow. As Little understood it, the review Curt thought "very good" perhaps missed a point in unstinted praise: "excellence thru grace of means . . the program might have taxed his only comparable elder over three times his age." That won't touch anybody one bit, Little thought very maturely, Oldman is hinting at his friend Ztephiah, who if he is curious will care less than his manager Endor.

As for the newspaper with the greater circulation it stung. Perhaps Little expected that its leading critic, who knew good playing from bad, so cavalier with the precise virtuosity of his nonage two years ago—and Little himself knew he had improved—would say, if only to show up less bald than Oldman, that the former child now has a mind of his own, and as for smiling the reviewer once gave him a clean slate for the future. Little could imagine some such remark his slightly stooped violinist's shoulders might shrug off if he had to make amends in the style of the reviewer. He was more than a bit jarred that the lead column was not about his recital. Timely as the weather the critic had written an informal piece: (informed by the grapevine) / At home in the blizzard / while hardy patricians played / to not too warm but an intimate few. / An unknown name—A.Gnith—reviewed Little—inconspicuously near the inside margin of the page. The minor notice, after listing the program, expressed "a question of psychology" in one sentence: "What motivated parents to expose a growing talent yet to be spared an empty hall, of all halls Great Hall whose warm audiences time out of mind comfort the great performers?" "Psych'n lice thyself," Little reverted to his tenderer years. *Psychology*, the one word Verchadet had fought before he was born and that brought cat's bristles to Dala's spine. His shock over, Little again felt for their duo of silence. "A. Gnith—Dala," he whispered tentatively.

Dala turned still not seeing, riddling backward as in a mirror, "a thing," he said, "the dishonesty. He should know us, I could *kill* him."

"*Gentle* Dala," Little said with superior irony as he squared to the height of Manawyddan in *The Mabinogion.* Verchadet forced a smile: "he," meaning Dala, "should go in for vaudeville—the legitimate stage. No, Mr Gnith need not know us, we'll see to it you avoid him, Mabinog von Chulnt." They would too. Who else, after his two asinine assertions of one irate subject, *I* could kill, *he* should know —tse-tse . . no honor to Sextus Empiricus? no ballet for Verchadet and Little? His thought bŏwed in a minuet going right into his act of old Leopold. "Raupenfliege so wie verbum, ohne Wetter, und so hin, und so weiter, Amadeus Allezeit!"

Nerves would not let him clown that night. To feel— want to, yet false? He stood at the window and with a finger melted its crystals recalled as it were to his eyes.

He had dozed then for an instant—after asking to hear The Fantasia!—to be startled beside himself — yet heard—Verchadet played each note so

evenly no rubato of Neitsnebur rippling at the
moon could steal from her

Rocking in Dala's rocker so comfortable, outgrow-
ing his undershirt hitching above his navel—unlike Athens poking his bōw at it Dala thought
'There had been little, and *there is Little*' playing
an 'early' tape of his own and saying, 'As to listening to yourself something there not now but something now not there'

The blizzard whirled faster and thicker woods of white
leaves.

Dr Gluillens or maybe his banker saying, death
and (it) taxes; eleemosynary, distracted sometimes to the arts. Not charity, Dala believed he
said—*Infernal revenue*

'I appreciate,' she (James Madison) said carefully with a sibilant *c* instead of her breath of a
laugh, 'your telling me. Do you indeed hurt? You
always say it as if it doesn't.' To which Verchadet
winked with accomplishment and added: 'The illness is human, but there aren't very many people
we ought to be disturbed by—being really never
sensitive when we're *around* others, that's what
he's trying to say.' 'That seems honest enough to
me,' James Madison agreed.

Gathering crystals at the sash

Joined in the storm James, Gwyn, Dea—welshing
to Welsh Llywarch Hen, Welshing Aneirin:

pye, you bed whom?
bed whom and whom. gone i' me. me ag'ōn.

air panicked   dire our aneirin
new night his score has   not a gododin.

Each now stood at a window—leaving two white and black,
—unaffected window: but even as they stood at the other

three, instead of black of the unlooked thru two iced deep blue. The blizzard stopped almost instantly after. "Dawn," Little said at his window, "and I'm not sleepy. There's a thin chalk dust out there blowing but not falling." Not very long the dawn reflected brilliantly in their west windows. "Today it will be lovely," Verchadet said, "no prima donna beats nature," and walking away from her window, "breakfast."

There was Dala's little table Little called *tabula rasa* at the window nearer the warmer wall, where his legs out of their way they breakfasted. "No path for the cow" (meaning milk) "today," Verchadet said, "since you stayed up all night, Little, coffee?" "It would be disgracious to refuse gifts," he said. She set it down for him. He took one wry sip. "Needs sugar," he said. "Not coffee," Verchadet said. He took another, and pushed the cup in its saucer a bit away from him, "Hot enough." "The omniscient observer," Dala said continuing for them out of another day, "reads from the first word to the last with great care for the spaces between them so they are unframed by enthusiasts or detractors. I read now—present tense—the moon is made out of magma." Little responded with a pizzicato in the air,

"Ex-plic-it,"

then with the ball of a finger of the same hand vibratoed on the wood of the table (for *good luck* Verchadet and Dala thought together) as on his instrument.

1950—July 28, 1969

The text face is Bodoni Book.
The composition and binding is by
H. Wolff Book Manufacturing Company, New York, N.Y.
The paper is by Monadnock Paper Mills, Bennington, N.H.
The printing is by Noble Offset Printers, New York, N.Y.
The design is by Jacqueline Schuman.

6